vindicated

| a Cedar Valley novel |

S. WAGNER

Line Editor & General Badass: Shawna Brown
Publisher: Six Bridges Press, LLC

ISBN: 979-8-9870471-3-2

CONTENT WARNING

This book contains elements that may be triggering or disturbing for some readers. If you feel triggered by any of the following, please don't proceed with reading this book.

Your mental health matters!

Alcohol Use

General Trauma

Death

Suicide

Stalking

Abuse

Weapons

Graphic Sexual Content

Profanity

| This book is not intended for anyone under the age of 18 |

To everyone looking for a safe place to call home.

Prologue

I check the time on my phone again as I pace back and forth between two trees. There are eight steps between them, six if I lengthen my stride. It's getting late and something is off. Charlotte never stays out this late, at least not since that stupid bitch, Nikki, finally moved away. I don't even care where she ended up. She was always in the way, butting her nose in where it didn't belong.

She's why I've been forced to do this for so long, watch and wait. I figured once Nikki was out of the picture, Charlotte and I could pick up where we left off, but she's been a little harder to convince than I expected. Turning me into the police for harassing her. Please. The police didn't believe her, which I had hoped would make her come to realize that she and I were meant to be together. That all of this harassing she was accusing me of doing was just in her head. But that's how a lot of things are when it comes to Charlotte, it's just all in her head.

My father always taught me it was important to have an obedient partner who respected you. And if they didn't respect you, well, then you needed to punish them and show them you are the one in control. I tried to handle things with Charlotte differently, but she just didn't get it.

I asked her not to wear certain things that made me look bad or act certain ways around my colleagues, but she just wouldn't listen to me. It's her own fault I had to punish her. If she would have just listened to me from the start, we wouldn't be in this situation. She's living her life like I don't exist, while I stand in a wooded area watching her from afar, like a ghost.

It's all your fault Charlotte, and I'm really going to enjoy giving you your next punishment.

CHAPTER 1

Charlie

"I'm done." I throw my head back, letting the liquid courage in a tiny shot glass roll down my throat. "I can't do this anymore. I'm going to sign up to be a nun. Do you know how I do that?"

"Let's not go that far, I think it's the alcohol talking." Nikki laughs and takes the shot glass out of my hand, shoving it toward the bartender while he chuckles along with her.

"You think this is funny and I'm being serious!" I mean it. I'm so over dealing with assholes. Why is it so difficult to find a decent man these days?

"You are not, you're just upset. But I'll tell you what, if you feel the same way in the morning, I'll start researching convents for you." Nikki winks at the bartender who smiles while rolling his eyes and moves down the bar to take care of someone else.

"Fine, we can reconvene in the morning." Resting my forehead on my palm I can't help but feel like something is wrong with me. Every little prick I end up dating screws me over one way or another.

My high school boyfriend, Ethan, was a complete idiot. He was far more into himself than he was me and I took too long to realize it. He spent more time getting ready than I did and cared way too much about what people thought of him. Then there was Alex. He was fine at first, and very attentive. He was the complete opposite of Ethan in that he could have cared less what people thought about him. But, once he got comfortable, all of the attentiveness turned into aggressiveness.

I was blinded by the attention after being so starved of it in my relationship with Ethan that at first, I didn't see what others saw with Alex. And once I finally came to my senses, things were out of control. When I finally left Alex, the controlling and abusive behavior turned into stalking and threats. Nikki insisted I pack up and move here, to Cedar Valley. That's the kind of friend Nikki is. She's kind and caring but not afraid to stand up for what she believes in or those she cares about. Most days I wish I could be more confident like her, more unafraid.

"Listen, Charlie, Dane was a dick, plain and simple. You did nothing wrong."

"I know, I know. It's just hard to think it's not something with me since I have the worst track record when it comes to relationships."

"I know it seems that way, but those guys just weren't meant for you," Nikki says, reassuringly. "You'll find the right one when it's the right time. Maybe just take some time for yourself for a bit, don't be done completely."

Nikki and her boyfriend, Ben, have been dating for years, and she's blessed. He's wonderful and treats her like a queen. She deserves nothing less. I wouldn't be surprised if he pops the question soon. He's been hinting at it. I always feel a tinge of jealousy when we all spend time together. I want someone who genuinely cares for me, like Ben does for Nikki. Today has just been… a day… and I want to forget it.

I can't get it to leave my brain no matter how hard I try. I wanted to surprise Dane today at his office for lunch. It *was* his birthday after all. His building is just a couple blocks away from my store, and Nikki offered to cover for me even though she can't stand Dane. She tells me his eyes wander when we're out, and it worries her. But, if he was anything like Alex, she definitely wouldn't be supportive of me surprising him.

It's the middle of July, and hot as hell outside, so I was extremely frustrated with how much I was sweating from the short walk. When I arrived at Dane's office, his assistant wasn't anywhere to be found so I walked past her desk and down the hall, figuring he might be on the phone or in a meeting. I knocked on the door lightly and, after no answer, I cracked it open. I felt like my retinas were burned when I saw him balls deep in his assistant, who was bent over the desk. I immediately ran out as fast as I could and into the street where I hurled into a trashcan. He followed me out, calling after me, but I just kept speed walking back to my store.

When I got back, I was a mess, and Nikki convinced me to close up early and go to O'Henry's with her for some drinks. I didn't have the ability to decline. It sounded way better than sitting somewhere he might find me.

"Can we get a couple more beers down here?" Nikki asks the bartender with a smile before turning back to me. "Look, I know it sucks, but it's better to find out now rather than later when you're married and have kids, don't you think?" I'm thankful she isn't throwing out *I told you so's,* even though she has every reason to.

"Yes, I know. And, if I'm being completely honest with myself, I think I knew this wasn't going anywhere. I had a feeling something was going on with how he'd been acting lately." I shrug my shoulders and let out a sigh. "He rarely wanted to spend time with me anymore and was always hiding his phone when I would walk into a room. And we'd only been seeing each other for a couple months."

"At least you weren't living together or more serious. It will be a pretty clean break. Ben will probably murder him when I fill him in later anyway, so you won't need to worry." Nikki shrugs and slides my freshly poured beer towards me. "Drink up! Tomorrow is your day off!"

As I begin to down my next beer, my mind wanders back to the last evening I spent with Alex.

CHAPTER 2

Charlie - past

Tonight is a big night for Alex, and I'm terrified that I'm going to fuck it up. The last time I screwed up at one of his work functions, I ended up in bed for a week with a black eye and bruised shoulder from his attack on me. I should have known better than to have a conversation with his colleague without him present but, I was kind of backed into a corner, and didn't want to be impolite. That would have also resulted in a punishment. I was able to put Nikki off after the attack. I didn't want her to become aware of how bad things had gotten. She would have called the police, and that attention is the last thing I need until I can get out of this situation.

I put on the red dress that Alex picked out for me and look at myself in the mirror. I turn to look at the back and notice the fingerprint bruises on the back of my upper arm. *Dammit.* I thought I covered those better. As I stare at them, I notice a reflection in the mirror behind me and see Alex standing in the doorway. I tense up and all of the nerves in my body electrify at the same time.

He moves towards me slowly and brushes his fingertips on the bruises. "I thought I told you to cover these?" I try not to flinch.

"I did but some of the makeup must have come off when I got dressed." I fumble for my foundation on the stand next to the mirror, trying not to let the rising bile in my throat escape. I hate when he touches me softly. I would rather him be hitting me, to be honest. At least then I don't feel like I'm going to throw up. "I'll fix it."

"I'll do it." He grabs the foundation bottle out of my hand and a sponge from the stand. As he applies the foundation, he hisses in my ear, "If you weren't so pale, your bruises wouldn't show so easily." Satisfied with his cover up, he turns me around to face him, looking me up and down then nodding in approval.

"Remember the rules." He places his hand on the small of my back, leads me out of the apartment and down to the waiting car.

The awards ceremony was going fine, and I was following all of Alex's rules, just like he asked. But I could tell he was upset when another employee got the award he had been banking on. His eyes always turned dark when he was angry, like soulless pools of black water. I remain calm and lean towards him, hoping not to push the wrong buttons in public.

"Would you like me to go get you a drink?" I ask in the sweetest voice someone can muster when speaking to a living, breathing, monster.

"That would be great." He gives me a tight smile and plays his part well. When people are watching, he's very careful. I walk over to the bar and order his favorite whiskey. As I'm waiting for the bartender, I feel a hand touch my back. I tense immediately and turn to look, only to realize it's not Alex touching me.

"Please don't touch me." I flinch and move a step to the side, hoping Alex is in a conversation at the table and not watching this happen.

"Are you here with someone?" The man asks, looking around the room.

I turn my head to look over my shoulder and see Alex's black stare glued on us at the bar. *Fuck. I'm in for it tonight.* I quickly grab the glass of whiskey from the bartender, along with the small silver object sitting just inches away from it, and head back to my seat next to Alex.

When I sit and slide the glass over to him, he leans towards me and whispers in my ear, "I warned you not to be a stupid whore."

He sits back in his seat and chugs his glass of whiskey while maintaining eye contact with me. I know better than to look away, so I watch him finish it and set it on the table.

"Let's go." He stands and escorts me out of the venue.

Alex doesn't say a word in the car, which is almost worse than when he yells at me. At least when he speaks, I know what's going through his head. But, when he turns silent, I know the punishment will be ten times worse.

When we arrive back at the apartment, he unlocks the door and lets me go in first. It takes everything in me to not turn and run away. I want to but I'm afraid of the consequences when he catches me. The worst he's ever done is hit me, so I prepare myself for the inevitable beating I'm about to receive for doing nothing.

He slams the door behind us, and I jump at the noise. All of my senses are on high alert, and I don't dare move from the spot I stand in the entryway. I can't move until he tells me what I can do. I know he's had enough whiskey that whatever he's about to do to me could be unpredictable.

He moves up behind me and wraps his arms around my waist, pinning me against him. "What did I tell you about flirting with my colleagues?" he asks, hissing in my ear.

"If I want to act like a whore then you'll treat me like a whore." My breath is shallow, and my knees are weak. I force myself to continue standing in his grasp.

"So, you want to be treated like a whore?" he asks, and I can feel his erection growing against my ass. *No!* I scream internally, but push it back down, knowing the result will be a harsher punishment.

"Yes." I whimper and a lone tear falls down my face. I will not let him see me cry, so I steel myself, and force the tears stinging the back of my eyes to disappear. I will not show weakness.

"Get on your knees." he says, and I do as I'm told. This is the best option for right now.

Once I'm on my knees, he walks around to face me, unzips his slacks, and frees his disgusting cock. The sight of it makes me want to vomit. He presses the tip against my lips, and I part them to obey his unspoken request. As he fills my mouth with his ugly ass dick his head falls back and his eyes close.

Now is my chance. Slowly, I take the cocktail fork I stole off the bar at the venue out of my bra and, in one swift motion, stab him in the thigh as hard as I can.

A guttural howl escapes his throat, and he pulls out of my mouth instantly, falling to the ground. I seize the opportunity, jump to my feet and head for the door, grabbing my clutch off the table. I rush out of the apartment, down the stairs and out the doors.

CHAPTER 3

Charlie

Oh. My. God. My head feels like it weighs 100 pounds, and I can't even open my eyes. I should not have drunk so much last night. Thank God my store is closed today. There's no way I could have made it in. I lean over, open my nightstand drawer, and grab out some pain relievers. I wash them down with an old bottle of water that's been sitting on top and pull the covers back over my head. I don't even care that it tastes like dirt.

I try to go back to sleep but that's not going to happen. My mind keeps reliving yesterday and I cannot get the mental image out of my head.

I reach out from under the covers and feel for my phone on the nightstand. I finally palm it and bring it under the blanket with me.

Fifteen missed calls, ten text messages, all from Dane. Perfect. There's no way I'm speaking to him today. I click on the messages.

I'm so sorry Charlie. Please call me.

Eye roll.

Charlie, we need to talk.

Nope.

Where are you? The store is locked up.

None of your fucking business, asshole.

Are you going to ignore me?

Yep.

Please call me.

Absolutely not.

Text me? Anything?

Dream on.

It wasn't what you think. Please.

Oh please.

Charlie, text me. This is ridiculous.

You're ridiculous.

I just want to know you're ok.

What the hell do you think?

Fine. Fuck this.

No. Fuck you.

I'm so glad Nikki took my phone last night or I'm sure I would have been drunk calling or texting the asshole. Now that I'm sober, I don't care if I ever speak to him again. For all I care, he can go kick rocks…barefoot.

There's a soft knock on my door. "Char, you up?" Nikki cracks the door and peaks in.

"Unfortunately." I stick my arm out from under the covers and hand her my phone without moving the blanket off my head. "Here."

She takes the phone out of my hand before moving over to the window and slinging open my blackout curtain, filling the room with an instant blinding light.

"What a douche," she says after reading the texts. "You're better off. Wanna go get coffee? It'll make you feel better."

"Yeah, let me shower first." Coffee sounds good. I sit up in bed and look around the room, my eyes still blurry. My clothes from the night before are strewn across the floor while half my pillows join them there, as well. Everything is knocked over on my dresser, presumably because I was feeling my way around in the dark when we got home last night, or a random raccoon made its way into my room. I'm going to put money on the racoon…I don't remember doing any of that.

"I told Ben what happened. He's livid. I'm not even sure they'll be friends after this." She sits on the edge of my bed, folding a random throw blanket, as I get up and head to the bathroom.

"Well, if they remain friends, I won't be around when he is." I shut the door behind me and hop in the shower. I turn the water to scalding hot. I need to wash all memories of yesterday off of me. What a fool I was to trust another man. They are all the same, well, all of the ones that are interested in me are, anyway. I'm just damaged goods with too much baggage. I'll never find someone like Ben. The only men who want me want to control me, and I'm done being controlled.

Daily's Coffee Shop is the best place in town to get good caffeine, unless you consider gas station coffee 'good'. It's a cute little shop two doors down from my bookstore, so Nikki and I are regulars. After grabbing our hangover cures from the barista, Nikki and I take our usual table at the back of the shop. I'm barely into my first sip before I notice a familiar face at the counter.

"Holy shit, don't turn around and don't draw attention to us." I lean my head down and try to cover my face with my hand. "This fucking small town."

"What?" Nikki mimics my failed attempt to hide while trying to look over her shoulder, sneaking a peek at the back of the customer at the counter. "Is that…?" She trails off looking back at me.

"Yep." My face reddens and all I can see is her bent over Dane's desk. I'll never be able to look at her any differently.

"Want me to say something?" Nikki whispers, sipping her coffee.

"Hell no!" I exclaim. Shit, that was too loud. The girl turns around and makes eye contact with me, almost jumping when she realizes who I am.

Fuck. She turns back around and grabs her coffee from the barista. *Please don't come over here.* She wouldn't, right?

"Shit, she's coming over here. Don't say anything." I say sharply to Nikki.

"Charlie?" Katie asks. She seems shyer than I imagined.

"It's Charlotte to you." Nikki snaps at her, scooting her chair back like she's going to stand up and get in her face.

I reach out and grab Nikki's hand to stop her. Nikki is a force and I'm one hundred percent sure Katie wouldn't survive.

"Katie." I stare at her, folding my arms over my chest.

"About yesterday, I…"

I put my hand up to stop her sentence. I don't need fake apologies. "Thank you."

"Thank you?" She seems puzzled, and rightfully so.

"Yes, thank you for showing me what I was getting myself into. Good luck with all that." I wave my hands in the air and chuckle. She doesn't say a word, just looks back and forth between Nikki and I, her hands visibly shaking as she holds her cup of coffee. As she begins to open her mouth to say something, Nikki stands and Katie steps back, turning and exiting the coffee shop just as fast as I walked out of Dane's office yesterday afternoon.

"The nerve." Nikki sits back down, and we both begin to laugh. "You seem to be doing better than last night."

"Yeah, I think you're right. It was better to find out now and I think I will take some time to myself for a while, work on getting the store finished up and just really figure out what I want."

"So, should I pause my research on convents?" she asks, winking at me.

"What?"

"Last night at O'Henry's? You said you wanted to be a nun?" She scrunches her forehead then laughs. "Oh…you don't remember."

Shaking my head, I close my eyes and try to remember the conversations from the night before. I remember bits and pieces but not everything.

"Fucking lemon drops!" We both sip our coffee and laugh, feeling a little lighter. "Wanna hit up the farmers market?"

"Absolutely!" Nikki smiles.

CHAPTER 4

Alex

It's been three months since I've seen Charlotte. Three months since I've watched her from a distance. Three months of going insane trying to locate her. You would think in this day and age, with such advanced technology, it wouldn't be so easy to disappear, but she's done just that. Even though I know her phone is no longer in service, it doesn't stop me from continuing to call it multiple times per day.

Some people might call me crazy for the lengths I have gone to in trying to locate Charlotte. I call it determined. She isn't going to get away from me that easily. I have put too much time and effort into that woman, and I'll be damned if she's going to make me look like a fool.

"Alex, how are the plans coming for the company outing next month?" I look up from my computer screen to see Gerard standing in the doorway of my office. He's a short and stocky man with soft, feminine features and an extremely punchable face. His personality isn't worth raving over either.

"Good, I've got the suite booked out for the game and Janine has the menu all set." Next month is our yearly company outing for all the branch offices within Bradford and Swartz Real Estate. We have 20 satellite offices located all over the country.

"I've been in touch with all of the branch leads and it seems like everything is good with all of them, as well." Gerard says. "Keep me updated if you need anything." He turns and leaves my office.

Finally. He's always interrupting my research.

I can't believe she deleted all of her social media accounts. If anyone is crazy, it's her. The police didn't even believe her when she tried to claim I was stalking her. Why would a high-profile real estate agent be stalking a nobody entrepreneur? My therapist says that I need to just let her go, but I refuse to do that. She also tells me to stop calling myself a real estate agent, but I pretty much do all their work as an assistant, anyway. I'm more tempted to let the therapist go. She's full of shit advice.

I have a friend down at the police station. I've been holding off calling him these past few months but I'm running out of options at this point, so I pick up the phone and dial his number. He answers on the second ring.

"Jacobsen."

"Long time no talk, buddy. It's Alex."

"Alex. How are you? Finally getting over that whole stalking mess from a while back?"

"Yeah, that was bogus, and you know it." I laugh, playing it off as best I can. "Listen, I need to get ahold of Charlotte. Some money came in for her after she left, and I haven't been able to get in touch with her to make sure she gets it. It seems her phone isn't working anymore. Is there any way you can try to locate her for me?"

"Oh…Alex…I don't know if that's a good idea. I know the charges she brought against you were dropped but that might look kind of sketchy on my end. I mean, I believe you didn't do anything wrong but the optics man, they wouldn't be good."

"I completely understand, it's just that this is a large sum of money and I'm sure she could probably use it." I can't believe this asshole, after everything I've done for him in the past. "You can do it quietly, no one has to know if you're worried about how it's going to look."

"Alright, I don't think it's a good idea, but I'll see what I can find." The line goes dead before I can thank him. I slam my fist down on the desk. *Dammit. This could have been a huge mistake.*

CHAPTER 5

Jude

I didn't really have time to be here today with everything going on at the jobsite, but it's really hard to say no to Hazel. She's been having some back issues and wasn't sure she could load everything into the truck by herself, and let's face it, I'm all she has.

"How many more boxes do we have to load?" I ask. There can't be many more, the truck bed is almost full.

"I've only got three left in the house full of soaps. If you want to grab those, we will be good to go." Hazel walks around the truck and gets in the passenger seat. She's not a frail woman by any means and reminds me of my grandma in a lot of ways. Hazel is a hard worker and doesn't take shit from anyone. Just how I like it. She's short and stocky, with working hands and dark skin from years out in the sun. Her hair is almost all gray now, not black like how I remember it as a kid.

I recall sitting on the porch with my brother, playing with our toys, while Grandma and Hazel sat and gossiped. They would talk about things going on in town or how Gertrude from down the road was caught with her farm hand in the barn by her husband one Sunday after church. They would laugh and tell me not to repeat anything I heard them say. I do miss those days and I definitely didn't repeat anything.

I run inside and grab the last of the boxes, setting them in the bed of the truck. "You've got quite a load this week, Hazel."

I hear her chuckle from the cab of the truck. "Oh, quit complaining. It's not more than you can handle! I've been keeping myself busy, isn't that what you want me to do?"

I hop in the truck next to her and start the engine, which takes a few seconds seeing as how this thing is older than I'm. "When are you going to get a new truck, Hazel? This thing is going to die on you someday and leave you stranded on the highway."

"Never. This truck was given to me by my daddy, and I don't plan to ever get rid of it. They don't make vehicles like they used to. This thing is solid." She smiles, patting the dashboard while I just shake my head and pull out of the driveway.

Hazel lives outside of town on a farm that has been in her family for four generations. The drive to town is winding and slow, much like the hills that surround the narrow gravel roads. It's quiet out here and that's how Hazel likes it. That's how I like it. I'm not a city guy and don't ever plan to be. I like my space and my privacy. That's why I hate the farmer's market. Too many people for my taste, and socializing, which I also hate. I don't like small talk, and for some reason, all the women in this town think I do.

Every time I show up to this farmer's market, Hazel makes a lot more money than if I don't, so I guess she doesn't mind the flock of women at the stand. I try to stick it out at least once a month to help Hazel make some extra money. It's the least I can do for everything she's done for me. That doesn't mean I have to enjoy it, though.

Just as I suspected, the market is busy today, and it seems like everyone in Cedar Valley is out and about this morning. I unload all of Hazel's items while she takes time setting up the table. She's good at making small talk as people pass by, definitely better than me. It's also probably why she has all the good dirt on everyone in town.

"That's the last one. Anything else you need?" I ask as I shut the tailgate on the truck.

"Just your handsome face. Hazel has property taxes due soon." She smirks at me and takes a seat in her lawn chair behind the table. Hazel makes the best goat milk soap in Cedar Valley. Well, it's the only goat milk soap in Cedar Valley, but everyone loves it. All the mom's rave about how great it is for their skin, and they love how natural it is. If I hear one more woman say the word 'organic,' I swear I might lose my shit.

"Good morning, Jude." I look up to see where the whiny, annoying voice is coming from even though I already know it's Kelsey Long. Ugh, I hate small talk, especially with her. Kelsey's not unattractive by any means, she's tall and thin with sharper features than most women, but generally not a bad catch for this town. It's the personality that's the unattractive part. Clingy women aren't my type. I like someone who is independent. Someone who wants me but doesn't need me.

"Good morning, Kelsey." I force a smile and hope it comes off as genuine, for Hazel's sake.

"How have you been?" She twirls her blonde hair between her fingers while she browses through the soaps on the table, pretending to be interested in them.

"Fine, and you?" She better purchase something if I have to endure this conversation.

"Good. Hey, I haven't heard from you for a few weeks, since that night at O'Henry's." She picks up another soap and smells, eyeing me from behind it.

"Sorry. Things have been…busy." It's not a lie. I have been busy. Busy avoiding her. This is what one too many beers at the local pub gets you. Bad decisions and regret.

"Well, if you get un-busy, give me a call sometime." She shifts her focus to Hazel. "I'll take two of these. I love that they're organic."

Fucking shit.

"That girl seems to have eyes for you, dear." Hazel smirks and raises one of her brows at me.

"Yeah, well, I'm not interested." I don't know how I can make it more clear to Kelsey. She just won't let it go. I definitely don't want to be rude but at some point, she's going to have to figure it out.

CHAPTER 6

Charlie

The farmer's market is busy today, seemingly busier than usual. I've only been a couple times since moving to Cedar Valley, but I do like to browse around and see what the locals have for sale.

"I hope Hazel is here today. I want to talk to her about putting some of her stuff in my store."

"You want to sell Hazel's soap in your bookstore?" Nikki looks at me confused.

"Yeah, of course. Most people who read are into more natural and health-conscious stuff. Plus, I've heard she's kind of struggling right now and I would like to help her out. I know how much her farm means to her."

"You amaze me, Char. You always focus on taking care of other people even when you've been kicked down." She shakes her head at me as we make our way down the aisles of stands.

There are fresh produce stands lined with fruits and vegetables. There are also lots of women selling homemade items like aprons, towels, baskets, and the occasional quilt. We find a stand making fresh smoothies and grab one. Nikki's right, I do love caring for other people, but I'm well aware someday I'm going to have to start thinking of myself more. I just don't like how selfish it makes me feel.

"Hazel's stand is down there." Nikki motions across the lane. "And dear God, who is that hottie at the stand with her?" Her mouth is visibly agape and she's fanning her face.

I finish paying for my smoothie and turn around. I've never seen him before, and even though it is a small town, I don't get out much.

"Never seen him before." I shrug as we make our way over to the stand. However, I can't help but notice him, but I try to hide my interest. *Snap out of it Charlie, you just swore yourself off of men.* Plus, he looks particularly unhappy, and I'm bound to attract that.

"Hey Hazel!" I smile as we approach. "How are you feeling today?" I purposefully attempt to ignore the man standing next to her. Good Lord, he's even more attractive up close. *Down girl.* He's well over six feet tall judging by how close his head is to hitting the tent Hazel has set up. His chiseled features are ones that make most women go weak in the knees. The veins in his arms are prominent with the heat blanketing Cedar Valley today. The sunglasses he's wearing have reflective lenses, telling me he's a bit standoff-ish when it comes to socializing.

"Oh, not too bad honey. My back is out so that's why I've got my handsome helper here." She smiles and nods towards the tall, rugged man standing next to her, who is leaning casually against the back of the truck. You could have pulled him right out of the pages of a farming magazine. His jeans hug him in all the right places and his white t-shirt sticks to him from the heat. I look over at him and smile. He smiles back but I can tell he's less than thrilled to be here.

"Don't be rude, introduce yourself to the lady." Hazel chastises the man, prompting him to stick out his hand to shake mine, after wiping it off on his jeans.

"Jude." He states, quickly shaking my hand. Nikki's eyes are as big as saucers and I'm not sure I've ever known her to be this quiet.

"Charlotte." I mimic his tone. Jeez, he's *friendly*. Ignoring the electricity in his handshake, I turn back to Hazel. "Listen, Hazel, I wanted to talk to you about some of your products. I would love to see what we could do to get some of your soap in my store."

"In your bookstore?" Hazel seems as confused as Nikki was.

"I really think my customers would love it, plus it would be extra income for you and more access for people to get their hands on your awesome stuff." I try to ignore the intense stare I feel coming from the man standing against the truck.

"I was confused too, Hazel," Nikki finally pipes up. *I see she can finally speak.* "But Charlie knows her stuff. It wouldn't hurt."

"You own the new bookstore?" Jude shifts on his feet, taking a sudden interest in our conversation. I glance in his direction but try not to maintain eye contact with him.

"She absolutely does! Have you been in yet?" Nikki sips her smoothie and smiles.

"I'm afraid I haven't." He shifts on his feet, again, and shoves his hands in his front pockets, drawing attention to his crotch. I realize I'm staring and turn quickly back to Hazel, hoping he didn't notice where my eyes landed through my sunglasses. *Get it together, Charlie.*

"Listen, honey. Why don't you come out to the farm tomorrow afternoon, and we can talk about this some more? I can make us afternoon tea." she winks, and I'm not exactly sure what she's insinuating, but I definitely want to help her, so I agree.

"Sure, I can come out tomorrow afternoon. How does two sound?"

"Perfect, honey. I'll see you then."

"Nice to meet you, Jude." Nikki grins, grabbing my arm as we leave Hazel's stand and continue to browse the market.

The way that man stared at me has me in all sorts of confusion. The intensity really threw me off. As we walk away, I can't help but still feel daggers being shot at me from behind, and against every bit of instinct left in my body, I quickly glance back over my shoulder towards Hazel's booth.

Fuck, he's watching me walk away.

CHAPTER 7

Jude

We packed up what was left from the farmer's market and headed back to Hazel's farm to unload everything. The ride back was pretty silent, and I couldn't stop thinking about Charlotte. I'm definitely not interested in getting involved with anyone, but it was odd to have a woman come to the booth and hardly even look at me, in the eye that is. She definitely didn't want me to notice she was glancing at my crotch, and I can't help but smile at the fact her sunglasses did little to hide her eyes. She should invest in some with reflective lenses if she's going to let her eyes wander so much.

Even with that, she seems different than most women around Cedar Valley. Her indifference towards me is not something I'm used to, and it caught me off guard a bit. Including the fact she seemed very intent on helping Hazel.

"How do you know the girl that owns the bookstore?" I ask hesitantly, regretting immediately after the words came out of my mouth.

Hazel smiles and looks over at me while I keep my eyes on the road in front of us. "Oh, you mean Charlie? She's a sweet girl. She moved here a few months ago. She didn't tell me everything, but I got the hint she was moving here for a fresh start. I ran into her at the farmers market a while back and we had a great talk. She told me she always dreamed of having her own business. So, I just put a bug in her ear that I had heard there was a building for rent on Main Street. Couple weeks later she found me at the farmers market and told me she was opening a bookstore."

"I see." I say, making sure not to look in Hazel's direction and keeping my eyes on the road. Still, I can't help but wonder why she would move out to the middle of nowhere.

"She's a pretty little thing, isn't she?" Hazel smiles, staring at me again from the passenger seat.

"I didn't notice."

"Mmhmm." Hazel nods her head, not believing me. She's smarter than I give her credit for, that's for sure. Obviously, I noticed. There aren't many attractive women in Cedar Valley, and I've pretty much met every single one there is. There's something different about Charlotte, but I would be a fool to try and figure it out.

After unloading the truck, I give Hazel a kiss on the cheek and head home. It's getting late but seeing as how it's July, the sun is just starting to set. I can't imagine living anywhere but here. It's so peaceful.

My farm is just a few miles down the road from Hazel's. I like being near her. Hazel is no spring chicken anymore and I need to be close to her in case something happens. I know for damn sure *he* isn't going to be here to help with anything. He made that clear years ago. However, I prefer it this way. I don't want him anywhere around me or Hazel. He's an ungrateful prick and we're both better off without him around.

I pull into the drive and Duke meets me out by the barn.

"Hey buddy." I greet him. He loves scratches behind the ears so, I oblige. He's a good boy, a basset hound I rescued from a local shelter a year ago. He's all I need to get by out here. Not that I don't get lonely sometimes. Kelsey, case in point. Damn that was a mistake. I should have known better than to get involved with her. It was only one time, and it didn't go any farther than a little dancing and getting handsy at the bar, but she wants more and that's the issue. *Stupid Jude.*

Charlotte on the other hand. I can't stop thinking about her. I know I came off a little rude, which wasn't on purpose. I was already frustrated by my conversation with Kelsey. Thinking back on it, I do feel bad, especially since she wants to help Hazel. I should stop in her store next time I'm in town and thank her for wanting to help, because that does mean a lot to me.

I gaze up at the hayloft in the barn. It always makes me nauseated, but I really need to get up there and clean it out. Maybe later this fall. I close up the barn doors and head inside. I need a shower and a beer. Too many people for one day.

CHAPTER 8

Alex

Perks of working for a real estate firm? Being able to rent properties easily. I've been working on my new apartment now for a few weeks. I need everything to be perfect for when I bring Charlotte back home. I also need to take her somewhere that she's never been. I can't risk her leaving again.

Cash is the only option when purchasing things that might raise a red flag to cops and store associates. I also make sure to purchase things sparsely and sporadically. I don't need to draw more attention to myself than Charlotte has already.

Today I grabbed some rope and duct tape but made sure to purchase them at different locations. Charlotte is going to need re-trained when I have her back in my possession and, after the shit she's already pulled,

I don't want to be left without any supplies I may need in the heat of the moment. The last thing I need is to have to run to the store because I was unprepared.

CHAPTER 9

Charlie

"Let's grab some takeout tonight and watch a movie." Nikki suggests as she gets into the car.

"Sounds great to me!" I could use some girl time after this shit show of a week.

"So, do you think Mr. Hottie will be at Hazel's tomorrow? Maybe I should tag along just in case." She smiles at me.

"Um, you have a boyfriend. And, I have no clue, plus I don't care. He was super rude anyway and I'm done with men. I told you that, remember?" I buckle my seatbelt and we head for home. "You also told me to take some time for myself, do you not remember that?"

Nikki offered me her spare room when she insisted I come to Cedar Valley after the incident with Alex. She had moved here for Ben a few months before and I couldn't think of a better place to start over than the middle of nowhere with my best friend. Nikki and I met in high school, and we've been inseparable ever since. Her house is small, and right at the edge of town, but it's big enough for what we need. She quit her job at the local cafe shortly after I opened the bookstore so she could start working with me there. I couldn't ask for a better person to spend most of my time with.

"Just because you're done with relationships doesn't mean you can't have a little fun once in a while. And I bet he knows how to have fun, if you know what I mean." She winks at me and nudges my shoulder, and I can't help but smile. She's not wrong, though. I might be done with men but that doesn't mean I don't have eyes. And the way he was staring at me was so intense.

"Yeah, yeah, "I say as I sigh and look out the window. "But that sounds messy and I'm getting really tired of everything being messy. I'm still on edge most days thinking Alex is going to pop up out of nowhere."

It's hard to even imagine being with anyone right now. I think I need to take a break and focus on myself. When I finally managed to escape Alex that night, I took an entire year to focus on myself. I spent that year finishing school and working a few dead-end jobs before ending up in Cedar Valley.

I remember collecting all my evidence against Alex and going down to the police station, only to be turned away because it wasn't enough for a restraining order. The justice system must be broken because I'm unsure how having that many texts and phone calls wouldn't be considered enough evidence. After getting no help at the police station, the texts and calls continued for weeks.

Then, one evening, I could see a figure standing near the tree line behind my apartment complex. I knew it was Alex and, in that moment, I realized he was never going to stop. The next day, I packed up every single belonging I had and left for Cedar Valley, with no plans to ever look back. I changed my phone number and deleted all of my social media accounts. I didn't want there to be any chance of him finding me.

The longer I'm in Cedar Valley though, the more comfortable I become. I feel more relaxed and safer as each day passes. But there's still a nagging feeling in my gut, and I'm having a hard time squashing it. Alex didn't like to be told no and I can't help but feel like he's not done with me yet.

"How about Chinese?" Nikki suggests, snapping me back to the present.

"Mmmm, sounds delicious." My mouth waters at the thought.

CHAPTER 10

Jude

Duke follows me into the house and to the fridge. I pull out a slice of cheese for him and a cold beer for myself. Cracking it open, I lean against the counter and smile down at Duke as he devours his treat in one bite. I look over at the sink full of dirty dishes and then at the pile of clean laundry on the couch. I really need to clean this place, there just aren't enough hours in the day.

"You should learn to savor your snacks, Duke." I'm pretty sure he behaves this way because he was so mistreated before I rescued him. He huffs at me in response, telling me he doesn't care what I think about how fast he eats his snacks.

I make my way back to the bedroom with my beer and sit on the edge of my bed, shoving another pile of clean laundry off to the side. At least it's clean. Duke follows and lays at my feet.

"Good boy." I take a long sip of my beer and lean forward, stretching my back. I know I'm not that old but carrying all of Hazel's stuff today didn't do me any favors. My phone chimes and I pull it out to read the text.

> It was really great to see you today.

Kelsey. I wish this woman could take a hint. I don't like to be rude to anyone but, it's getting to the point I may have to be in order to get her to back off. I thought, by being short in my replies to her, she would eventually move on and find someone else. I'm realizing that tactic isn't working. I need to end this once and for all.

> It was good to see you too. Listen, Kelsey, you're great but I'm just not in a position to be in a relationship with anyone right now. And I don't know if I ever will be, so stop wasting your time on me.

I hit send and hope I was clear enough. I throw my phone on the bed and head to the shower with my beer in hand. If there's one thing I do have time for, it's a shower beer.

My bathroom is one of the most modern rooms in this old farmhouse. I remodeled it soon after moving back in because some of the old water pipes busted and flooded half of the house. I chose to go with dark, almost black, stone tiles for the shower. I wanted something rustic but clean, and easy to take care of at the same time. The rest of the room is in natural woods and whites, with gold accents. The large soaker tub I installed in the corner was probably a waste, I've never used it, but it's nice to have the option. I have no plans of ever leaving this home, so I designed the bathroom, and the other rooms I had to remodel, so I would have a space I like and enjoy being in.

I toss my clothes on the floor, vaguely realizing I keep making piles of random laundry all over the house and hop in the shower. Letting the hot water cascade down my face and over my chest, my thoughts return to Charlotte. Her dark hair and piercing blue eyes flood my mind, and I can't help but feel my cock start to get hard. What is it about her? It's not just the way she looks that I can't get out of my head, not that it doesn't help. She looked stunning in her simple outfit of jean shorts and a tank top, natural and not overdone with makeup and hairspray. There's also the way she carries herself, and how compassionate she seems. I haven't met anyone like that in a long time.

Against my better judgment, I let my imagination take over. I begin to pump my fist up and down my cock, thinking about how it would feel to have her lips wrapped around me. I might not be ready for a relationship right now, but there's nothing wrong with fucking my own hand.

CHAPTER 11

Charlie

I've only been out to Hazel's farm once since moving to Cedar Valley, but I love the drive. It's peaceful out here and the rolling hills make the drive worth taking slow, even though there's no way you could take it fast safely.

I grew up in the city and as a child I never would have imagined living in a place like this. The longer I'm here, I can't help but feel like maybe I belong here. I love the slower pace of life and how most of the people you run into are kind and friendly. *Most of them.* Even then, I can't help but feel a little anxious about visiting Hazel today. Not because of her, of course, but because of *him.* The last time I was here he wasn't, so maybe I'll get lucky. Or, maybe I won't, and he will be helping Hazel because of her health issues.

I sigh, turning onto her winding road and rolling the window down for some fresh air. It's another hot day but I don't care. I like the heat. As I pull into Hazel's driveway, I see her sitting on the porch in her rocking chair, waving at me. She's such a sweet soul.

I park and exit my car. "Hey Hazel."

"Hi honey, hot one today, isn't it?" She wipes her forehead.

"It sure is, but I like it." Taking the rocking chair next to her, she reaches over and pats my hand.

"So, should I get us some tea and we can discuss your offer?" She stands and heads for the door. I notice it's not very easy for her to get up and moving, even more so than the last time I was here.

"Sounds good to me." I say as she disappears inside.

After a moment, Hazel returns with two ice cold beers.

"Tea, huh?" I laugh.

"I hate to discuss business without *tea*, dear." She smiles, handing me one of the bottles, and slowly sits back down in her rocking chair.

"You know, I've enjoyed many afternoon teas on this porch," she says staring off into the distance. "My dear friend Betty and I would spend Sunday afternoons on this porch after church, chatting and laughing while the boys played here, right at our feet." She motions at the floor right in front of us. "We would sit for hours, just enjoying the view and each other's company. Having you here reminds me of those times and how I've missed having a friend to enjoy this porch, and *tea*, with."

It makes me smile. I hope someday, when Nikki and I are older, we can look back on our times together with such fondness. "Betty sounds like a wonderful lady."

"Oh, she was, honey. One of the best you'd ever come across. She got sick when the boys were teenagers. It was really hard on them. When she passed, I took the boys in. They probably could have taken care of themselves, but I didn't think I would be doing right by Betty to just leave them out on that farm all alone. So, the boys moved in here until they were old enough to be out on their own."

"What a wonderful thing for you to do for Betty's sons." Hazel amazes me more each time I talk with her. She's such a selfless person with a good heart. You don't find that in the city. People are too consumed with themselves to care about others.

"Oh no dear, not her sons. Her grandsons. She was raising them, after the accident, that is." She continues rocking in her chair and sipping her beer. "See, their dad was killed in a farming accident. Ran over himself with a tractor one afternoon. Their mother came home from the general store and found him. By the time the paramedics could get out here, it was too late. Such a tragedy. Then, not six months later, Jude came home and found his mama, Margaret. I think she just couldn't take it anymore alone, running the farm, the boys. It was a lot for her to handle by herself and I know Betty said she had struggled with depression after Bill's passing. Poor Jude, finding his mother like that. No child should ever have to go through that."

"Jude? From the farmer's market yesterday?" I try wrapping my head around what Hazel just revealed to me. Jude found his mother? I can't even imagine what that would do to a young boy, losing both parents so close together.

"Yes, dear. Jude and Dane. Jude had a really rough time, but he's got a soft heart. Dane, he stuck around until he was old enough to get out of here, and get out of here he did. That boy has always been like stone and hated being out here on the farm. Well, hated it after his mama died, anyway. He and Jude don't see eye-to-eye on a lot of things, and I don't think they even speak anymore. Heck, I haven't seen Dane in probably five years, maybe six."

I freeze and don't even realize I've stopped rocking in my chair.

Dane.

Jude.

Brothers?

They aren't kidding when they talk about small towns. Dane didn't even mention he had a brother.

"You okay, honey? You look a little pale." Hazel chuckles.

"Um, yeah…yeah. I'm good. Can we talk about the store perhaps? I really would love to offer your products to my customers." I say, needing to change the subject. I'll have to unpack this bombshell later.

"Absolutely dear, sorry for going off on that tangent. Tell me what you were thinking."

"A lot of the people who come into my store are very health conscious and even though it is a bookstore, I would like to put some of your items out and see how they do. I don't want to take a commission from you, I just want to test it and see if we get anything to sell. I have the perfect spot for a small stand right at the front so people will be able to see it from the street. We can start with just a few, see what happens, and then add more if it goes well. You would get more exposure than just going to the farmers market on Saturdays and it would be year-round instead of just during the warmer months."

"I think that would be fine with me, dear. But I can't let you not take a commission from me. It wouldn't be right."

"What if we try it first without a commission and if it does well, then we can work out a commission plan?"

"Only if you promise that will be the case. I don't want to take advantage of you or your generosity."

"Hazel, this is my offer. You are not taking advantage of me."

"Alright, dear." Hazel says, sticking out her hand to me. "Then we must shake on it to make it official. I'll get Jude to drop off some stuff for you this week."

Perfect.

CHAPTER 12

Alex

It's been longer than I had hoped and still no word from Jacobsen. With all of the resources he has at his disposal, you would think he would have been able to find something. I'm starting to get impatient.

"Jacobsen." He says after he answers on the first ring this time. Every other time I've called over the last couple days I've had to leave a message.

"It's about time. I've been calling."

"Alex."

"Did you find anything?"

"I've been trying to verify the number I found but I'm having some trouble. Didn't want to give you the wrong information."

"You found a number? That's great! Go ahead and give it to me, I'll verify it." I don't need him digging any further. If it's a wrong number, I'm sure I can figure that out for myself. The less attention I draw from people at the station, the better. I know they didn't believe Charlotte when she first contacted them about me but, if they find out I'm sniffing around trying to find her, they could start thinking differently of me. That's not what I need right now.

"Um, alright, if you're sure. But listen, you didn't get this number from me. Understand?"

"Absolutely. We never spoke. Now, what's the number?" I copy it down, thank Jacobsen and hang up the phone. Bingo. *Found you, bitch.* I rub the small scar on the outside of my left thigh and the rage begins to boil inside me.

CHAPTER 13

Jude

I have to run to the job site today and check on my guys, so I make a stop at Hazel's before heading toward town. I purchased the dilapidated motel on the edge of town about a year ago. The construction company I own had just finished a big job, and I was looking for something to keep the guys and myself busy for the summer. Usually, I renovate buildings and then turn them over for a profit, but I've decided to hold onto the motel for some residual income.

When I pull up the driveway, Hazel is sitting on her porch in her rocking chair.

"Beautiful morning, honey," she says, waving at me as I get out of my truck.

"It's going to be another hot one according to the weather this morning." I join her on the porch and sit in the other rocker.

"Can I get you some tea, dear?" She begins to stand, and I pat her arm with my hand.

"No, I'm good, Hazel. It's a little early for tea anyway. I just wanted to stop and check on you since I was headed into town. I have to go check on the guys today."

"How's the project coming? Are you going to be able to open on time?"

"The guys are moving along nicely. I think we'll be able to meet the opening date we hoped for."

"The motel will be a nice addition to the community. It was run down for so long, it's nice to see it being renovated. You're doing a great job and a great thing for Cedar Valley. Have you thought of a name yet?"

"No, I haven't. I've been toying with some ideas, though."

"That's good, honey, because you'll need a name to open." She winks at me and smiles. "Since you are headed to town, would you be willing to do ol' Hazel a favor?"

"Sure, what do you need?"

"Could you take a couple boxes of my things and drop them off at Charlie's bookstore?" She motions over to the boxes sitting on the edge of the porch. "Would save me a trip and my back."

"Of course, Hazel. I can do that. Do you need anything else while I'm out?" I stand and grab the boxes to load them into the truck.

"No dear. Thank you."

I toss the boxes in the back seat and wave to her as I hop in the truck and head to town.

I said I would stop in to see Charlotte's bookstore when we spoke at the Farmer's Market and dropping off Hazel's stuff gives me the perfect excuse to do so. I can't get her off my mind, and I'm not going to pass up an easy excuse to talk with her again. This whole situation goes against my better judgment but she's so damn intriguing it's almost annoying.

Pulling up to the front of the store, I'm impressed with what she has done to the building so quickly. The front is painted black with natural wood accents, and the iron sign out front spells out *The Book Nook* in cursive. I can't help but smile at the fact we have similar design tastes.

Inside the walls are a dark green and the same natural wood is used on the bookshelves. There is a sitting area to the left with a plush couch and two chairs surrounding a live edge, round coffee table. The store smells of old books and wood, nothing floral and girly like I imagined. I've never been a book guy, but this kind of atmosphere could almost make me pick one up.

"I'll be right out!" I hear her call from the back. I walk towards the counter at the back of the store as she walks out.

"Oh, hey…Jude? Right?" She smiles, setting her coffee cup down on the counter. She's dressed less casually today in a flowing yellow dress adorned with daisies. Her dark hair is pulled back into a high ponytail, accentuating her features even more.

"Right." Jeez, she didn't even remember my name and here I'm fantasizing about her when I shower. I snap myself out of my wandering thoughts. "Where do you want these? Hazel asked me to drop them by since I was already headed to town."

"You can just set them down there and I'll take care of it. Thanks so much for bringing them in."

"I should be thanking you for helping Hazel. It means a lot to me." Hazel has had trouble keeping up on her property taxes lately and I know some extra income would be good for her. Selling items at the Farmer's Market just isn't going to cut it anymore, I'm afraid.

"It's really my pleasure. I'm very fond of Hazel." She smiles, picking her coffee cup back up and taking a sip, looking at me through her lashes. *Fuck me.* She's gorgeous. My eyes trace a line from her ear down to her collarbone and then lower…

"What?" she asks, snapping me back to reality. I realize I've been staring far too long, and it was far too obvious.

Ding. The bell rings as the door to the store opens, saving me from my embarrassment, and Nikki walks in.

"Well, good morning, Jude. It's nice to see you again," she muses as she makes her way back to us.

"Nice to see you too, Nikki." I turn back to Charlotte, "Well, I better get going. I need to go check on the guys at my job site." She walks with me toward the front of the store.

"What kind of job site?"

"I'm renovating the motel on the edge of town."

"Oh, I've wondered who was doing that. It's looking really good. I think it will be great for the community."

"Yeah, I think so too." As we get closer to the door I stop and turn to her. "I love what you've done with the place. You have really great taste. Did you do all this yourself?"

"Oh, thank you, yeah…I like to do most stuff on my own if I'm able. I'll leave the plumbing and electrical to the professionals, though." She laughs and I can't help but stare again. I smile at her. *Get it together, Jude.*

"I might have to get some advice when it comes to the interior of the motel, I mean, if you'd be interested?"

"Seriously? Wow, I'd love to." She tucks her hair behind her ear and her blue eyes light up.

"Great. We can talk more later. Thanks again for helping Hazel. I appreciate it, Charlotte."

"Please, call me Charlie," she requests as I leave the store more confused and intrigued than when I arrived. What is wrong with me? *She's just a woman Jude. Get a grip.*

The guys are coming along nicely with the motel renovations, and we seem to be on track with all the projects we're juggling. The plumbers have finished what needed to be renovated and changed to abide by city codes, and the final walk through with the inspectors is scheduled for Wednesday.

"Hey boss," Kyle, one of my guys, says as we walk through the last room. "I think we will be ready for the electrician by the end of the week."

"Great, I'll call and get him on the books," I reply.

Once the electrical is done and inspected, we will be ready to finish up the drywall repairs, then we can keep moving forward with finishing touches. It's nice to be getting close to the end of this project. We walk outside where some of my other guys are taking a break.

"Looks like we will be on track boys, thanks for all the hard work."

"You bet, boss. Why don't you come with us to O'Henry's tonight for some beers? Celebrate a bit?" Rod asks as he throws his cigarette down on the ground and smudges it out with his foot.

"You know the boss doesn't like to go drinking with us." Kyle smacks me on the arm. He's not wrong. I don't like to mix business with pleasure often, especially when I'm the authority figure over these guys. "Probably for the best anyway. Not sure the old man can hang with us."

"Excuse me? I'm not that much older than you, asshole." *Kid's got some nerve.*

"I heard Charlie's single. Maybe we will run into her." Rod grins over at Kyle.

"Oh really. I've been trying to get her to go out with me since she moved to town, but she's been playing hard to get. She just doesn't know what she's missing out on." Kyle shoots him a glare. "Don't get any ideas Rod, I call dibs."

"Dibs? That girl wants nothing to do with you." Rod shakes his head.

"You'll see. I'll get her." Kyle says, confidently.

Over my dead body.

CHAPTER 14

Charlie

"I'm starving, what time is Ben supposed to pick us up?" I haven't eaten since breakfast. After seeing Jude today at the store my appetite was all out of whack, so I opted for a banana for lunch and am beginning to regret not having something with a little more substance.

"He said five thirty so he should be here any minute," Nikki said. She suggested going to O'Henry's with her and Ben tonight. I figured it was better than staying home alone and trying to find something to make myself for dinner. O'Henry's is really the only place to eat around here unless you want Chinese, or to drive a half hour to the next closest town.

I chose my favorite pair of ripped jeans and a black tee. I've really enjoyed being able to dress more casually since moving here. When I was with Alex, I was forced to look a certain way if we went anywhere, and if I didn't look how he deemed appropriate when we were out, he would definitely punish me for it.

"He's here!" Nikki shouts from the kitchen.

"Coming." I grab my bag and shoes and meet them both in the kitchen. "Hey Ben, thanks for picking us up."

"Of course, you two usually need a chaperone anyway." Ben smirks and Nikki shoves him in the shoulder.

"We do just fine without you," she says, winking at me and grabs her own bag off the hook.

"Mmmhmm. Sure you do." Ben isn't convinced and I don't blame him. He's been our designated driver on more than a few occasions. "Ready?"

"Let's go." I finish slipping on my tennis shoes and follow Ben and Nikki out the door.

O'Henry's is pretty busy for a Wednesday evening, and I already noticed Kyle is at the end of the bar glancing my way. *Wonderful.* I plan to avoid him like the plague if possible.

"Great," I say, leaning towards Nikki. "*Kyle's* here."

Nikki glances over her shoulder and rolls her eyes when she turns back to Ben and me.

"He's a douchebag." Nikki thinks almost every man is a douchebag, but she's not wrong about Kyle. He's a regular at O'Henry's and it seems like he hits on everyone. He's been persistent with me in the past, but I've been pretty good at keeping him at bay. As long as you don't get stuck alone with him, he's harmless.

"What are you going to order?" I ask while scanning the menu. O'Henry's serves the best pub food in town, well, the only pub food in town. "I think I'm going to do the fish'n chips."

"I was actually thinking the same thing!" Nikki closes her menu and looks across the table at Ben. "You gonna order the same as us, too?"

"No, I'm just going to get a burger." Ben smiles. "You weirdos order the same shit all the time. It's strange." He shakes his head as the waitress walks towards us with our beers.

As soon as she finishes taking our order and grabs the menus from us, Nikki pipes up. "So, Ben, guess who came into the bookstore today?"

I rub my face with my palms. "Seriously, Nikki. Do we have to do this?

"Uh huh, absolutely we do." She nods her head while smiling at Ben. "Take a guess."

"Hmmmm, please don't tell me Dane. I told him to stay away from you." He looks at me with concern in his eyes.

"Nope. Guess again." Nikki claps her hands together looking back and forth between Ben and me.

"Hazel?"

"Nope."

"Oh, come on, just tell me already." Ben gets frustrated with Nikki's games sometimes.

"Jude." She's smiling from ear to ear, clearly amused by her revelation.

"Jude?" Ben appears to be shocked. His mouth is parted, and his eyes are darting between the two of us. "What the hell for?"

"He was just bringing Hazel's stuff to the store," I say. "Stop making it more than it is, Nikki. I told you, I'm not interested."

"I know you keep saying that, but judging by the way he was looking at you today, I don't think we can say the same thing for him. He was totally into you. I could feel the heat radiating between you two and I was clear at the back of the store."

"Jude and Dane are complete opposites. I don't know how they were both raised by Betty and Hazel. I know Dane and I are, or were, friends. But, if you had to pick one, Jude would be it," Ben says, taking a sip of his beer and seemingly contemplating what he's going to say next. It seems like he's having trouble finding the right words. "Things happened…in the past. And it's not my place to say, but there's a lot you don't know. So, just tread carefully."

"How have you never mentioned Jude before?" Nikki asks, sounding annoyed with Ben.

"Dane never wanted to talk about him and asked me to not say anything, so I didn't. I don't know Jude that well, other than the fact he likes his privacy." Ben spins his beer glass slowly in his hand, avoiding eye contact with Nikki.

I always take Ben's advice seriously. We've became really good friends since he and Nikki got together. I can't help but be curious about what he means by *there's a lot I don't know*.

"Wait, you mean with their parents dying? Hazel told me about that." That's all I can come up with. I don't know much about either of them, but I do know that.

"No. Obviously that probably plays a part in all of this, but there's more. I just don't feel right saying something," Ben says and the table falls silent as I contemplate what he just told us. The evening now feels heavy and that's not what I wanted to achieve by going out tonight.

We finish our meals and order another round of drinks.

"I'm going to use the restroom," I say. I stand, and as I head down the hallway at the back of the bar, my phone chimes with an incoming text.

You can't hide forever.

My breathing quickens and I feel like my heart is going to explode out of my chest. My ears begin ringing and I can feel sweat building up on the back of my neck. I keep pace towards the restroom when I hear a familiar voice behind me.

"Charlie. Wait up."

I pause, sigh, and turn around. "What do you want, Kyle?" I don't try to hide the irritation in my voice. I could care less if he notices. I don't have time for his nonsense right now.

"Don't be like that, Charlie. I just wanna talk." He moves closer, too close, and I take a step back. He throws up his hands as if to surrender. "When are you going to let me take you out?"

I roll my eyes and try to contain my laughter. "I'm not interested, Kyle, and I have told you this countless times." Why can't men just take no for an answer? He takes another step forward and I follow suit by taking another step back. "Stop. Just leave me alone, Kyle. Take a hint. I'm not interested in going out with you. Ever."

This time, he takes three rushing steps towards me, and I trip over my feet, slamming into the side of the wall. Flashbacks of Alex swarm in my vision.

"Back off, Kyle." I hear his deep voice before I see him. "She said to leave her alone, so I suggest you do so."

Kyle turns on his heels to face Jude. "Stay the fuck out of it, boss. This doesn't concern you," he spits back.

"Maybe not, but when a lady asks you to leave her alone, you should listen." Jude moves closer to him, towering over him by a good six inches. I knew Jude was tall, but it's more obvious now. I move towards the restroom door as they get closer to each other. I don't know what's going to happen, but I don't want to be anywhere near it if punches start flying.

"Leave." Jude demands one more time before Kyle looks over his shoulder at me.

"Fuck this. I'm out Charlie." He leaves us alone in the hallway and I hear the front door of O'Henry's open, and slam shut. I relax as soon as I know he's out of the bar.

"Are you okay?" Jude moves closer to me and grabs my shoulders. I flinch at the bolts of electricity that course through me with his sudden contact.

"Yeah. I am. You didn't have to do that. I can handle him." I glance over his shoulder. "Why did he call you boss?" He moves his hands down my arms and a chill runs down my spine.

"You shouldn't have to handle him. He's one of the guys on my jobsite, however, tomorrow he's jobless." He hesitates for a second, like he's about to continue talking but instead closes the gap between us, grabs my face with his palms and lowers his mouth to mine. I should pull away but for some reason I can't explain, I don't. I let him kiss me for what feels like not long enough, but forever at the same time, before he pulls away. He takes a step back.

"I...I'm..." He struggles to find words.

I lurch forward and grab his t-shirt with my fists, tugging him back towards me. This time I'm in control and I kiss him again. *What the hell am I doing?* The alcohol is definitely affecting my judgment right now. I search for his tongue with mine, not holding back. His hands reach down and grab my hips, pulling me as close to him as I can possibly get.

I've never been kissed like this before. There's something more behind it. Need. Longing. Loneliness. I can't put my finger on it, but I'm also having a hard time focusing. I shouldn't be doing this but, at the same time it's the only thing that's felt right for me in a long time. I wonder if he can feel how hard my heart is pounding in my chest. I hope not but, then again, do I care?

"Ehemm." I hear a throat clear behind us, snapping me back to reality. I jump away, staring at Jude and then around him to see who is probably wanting to use the restroom behind me. *Nikki.*

She moves towards us, slapping Jude on the back and then grabbing my arm and pulling me towards the restroom with her.

"It's about fucking time." She smiles over her shoulder at Jude as the door shuts behind her.

"Bitch, what the fuck was that?" She screeches. "I was getting worried about how long you were in the restroom, but it seems you were doing just fine!"

"I...I don't know. It happened so quickly." I can still feel him on my lips. They are on fire. I place my index finger on my bottom lip trying to figure out what just happened. "One second Kyle had me backed into the corner and the next, Jude was kissing me." I stare at Nikki, my fingers still on my lips. "This is so bad. He's Dane's brother. I can't do this."

"Why the hell not? Of course you can. You just had the wrong brother the first time." Nikki washes her hands and looks at me through the mirror. "Tell me it was good? Yeah?"

I can't contain my laughter. "It was so good."

Looking at her reflection, I've never been more thankful for her friendship. She always knows how to lighten the mood and make me feel better.

"And you're still not interested?" She smiles back at my reflection in the mirror, and I don't know how to answer that question now. Thirty minutes ago, at the table, I was one hundred percent against this and now...well now I don't know what I am. I only attract terrible men, which can only mean that Jude will inevitably be terrible, even if he isn't right this second. That's how they all end up.

As we exit the restroom, the nauseating feeling returns to the pit of my stomach when I remember the text that came through just minutes before.

CHAPTER 15

Alex

I'm still unsure if I have the right number for Charlotte and I doubt she will reply to my message. I probably should have started with something a little less frightening, but I want her to know I will stop at nothing to find her. She's not going to get away with making me look like an idiot.

The whiskey has been flowing tonight after getting the number from Jacobsen earlier today. I played with that sticky note so much I almost rubbed off the number. Luckily, it was still legible when I decided to put it into my phone and fire off that text. It's late, and I can't help but wonder what Charlotte is doing right now. Hell, that's my new routine since she left without a trace.

Every evening is the same. I get off work and stop at the local cigar bar for a whiskey and smoke, before stopping at the liquor store. I grab a bottle of my favorite whiskey, take a cab to my apartment, where I pour a glass and sift through the photos in my phone that I took from the wooded area behind Charlotte's apartment building. I have photos of her in her room, on her balcony, in her living room, changing clothes and even cooking dinner for herself. She never knew I was watching her from the woods. Well, at least I thought she didn't. Stupid bitch never closed her curtains or blinds. She left everything open where anyone could see everything. She was asking for it.

After I look through all of my photos, I start my research. Tonight is a better night than most because I have my first lead to her whereabouts. I pick up the shiny little cocktail fork sitting on the end table next to my glass of whiskey and twirl it between my fingers. Such a tiny object that has caused so much pain. It's time to bring Charlotte home.

CHAPTER 16

Jude

I shouldn't have kissed Charlie at the bar last night but something in me snapped when I saw her backed into the corner. After the tension I was feeling at the bookstore earlier in the day, I hadn't been able to get her out of my head. Seeing that douchebag, Kyle, invading her space, I couldn't help myself.

Clearly, she can take care of herself, and I probably should have let her do just that. Normally, I'm not the one to make the first move, not since Katie. I really thought she was the one and it's taken me quite a while to heal from the trauma she and Dane have caused me.

I'm really frustrated with the push and pull going on in my head. I shouldn't be getting involved with Charlie at all but there's just something about that damn woman. I can't get her out of my head.

I'm afraid of the consequences if I can't give her what she needs. One of us will end up getting hurt, and I'm not in the business of hurting people. Especially Charlie.

Today, I'm headed to the jobsite to make some decisions for the motel. In order to meet our grand opening date, I need to decide on some of the fixtures and designs to be able to get them ordered and here in time. Charlie seemed interested when I asked her about helping me with some of the interiors, so I decide to stop by the bookstore to see if she has some time to take a look with me.

"Heyyyyy, Juude." Nikki sings to me as I enter the bookstore.

"I've never heard that before," I say sarcastically and roll my eyes as Charlie comes out of the back of the store.

"Jude. What brings you in today?" She smiles and those gorgeous eyes light up the way I like.

"I need to make some decisions on the finishing touches of the motel today, so I wanted to see if you had some time to look over things with me. That is, if you are still interested?"

"Oh, you were serious." She fiddles with her hands in front of her and looks to Nikki for reassurance.

"I don't say anything I don't mean." I stare into her eyes and lean against the counter.

"Oh…ummm…ok, yeah. Nikki, could you cover for me?" She hesitates, turning back to Nikki who is grinning from ear to ear as she scans books into the computer.

"Of course I can." She winks at me and looks back at Charlie. "I'll finish up getting the new books entered into the system while you are out."

"Thank you, I appreciate it. Should we go then? I just need to grab my bag." She points her thumb over her shoulder toward the back office.

"Sounds good." Turning to Nikki, I tap the top of the counter. "Thank you for covering for her."

Nikki just grins and nods as we leave the store.

"It's so muggy here." Charlotte fidgets in the seat next to me on our drive to the motel.

"It is." I agree. Something feels off and I can't help but think this awkwardness is stemming from last night's hallway kiss.

Silence fills the truck and I'm not sure how much more of this I can take. I run multiple scenarios through my head on how to cut the tension, and all my stupid brain comes up with is, "Do you want to talk about last night?"

Her head snaps in my direction. "Do you?"

"Not really." I respond. Fuck, why did I even bring it up. She simply nods her head in response, and we sit in silence for the rest of the drive.

"I really like the white penny tiles for the bathrooms. They are classic, but elegant." Charlie points at the tile board laying out on the table.

"I agree." Smiling, I walk around the table to look at the wall tile options. I wonder if she will choose my favorite this time, as well. "For the wall, do you think white again or something different?"

She walks around the table to stand beside me. One hand on her hip and the other scratching her forehead. She seems unsure.

"Well, what are your thoughts?" She looks up at me through her lashes. *Dammit.*

"I want to hear your opinion before I give mine." I stand crossing my arms and staring at her intently. I need to quit making a habit of staring at her, it's probably coming off creepy, but I can't help it. Every time I do, it sends chills down my spine, and I don't hate how that feels.

"Well, I guess I would go with this tan colored one if it were up to me," she says and points to the one I assumed she would pick. "It's still neutral but won't make the bathroom feel so sterile. It will bring warmth into the space, and make it feel more like home."

"I couldn't have said it better. Tan it is." We've been looking at different finishes for the last couple hours and I'm really pleased with what we've decided on.

We chose black fixtures for the bathrooms to complement the neutral tiles. For curtains, we went with a beige blackout and a white drapery overlay to give the guests options when it comes to how much light they want in the room. We chose a linen textured wallpaper for the main spaces of the rooms, and a warm wooden flooring to use throughout the entire motel.

"I think it's going to be so beautiful when you're done. I might have to book a room just to try it out when you open." She smiles and turns to face me. "If we're done, I better be getting back to the store. I hate to leave Nikki alone for too long." Her phone chimes with an incoming text and I can't help but notice that her hand starts shaking when she reads it. She quickly shoves the phone in her back pocket.

"Everything okay?" I don't like the uneasy feeling I'm getting from her all of a sudden. Something in that text threw off the whole energy in the room.

"Um, yeah…yeah, totally fine. We should go." She stutters and gets fidgety. I'm positive she's lying to me, but it's not my place to question her, so I don't.

I had such a nice time with her this afternoon. I don't want to ruin it by pushing buttons I have no business pushing. It's been a long time since I've been so at ease with a woman. It probably helps that she isn't trying to jump me at every chance she gets, even though I wish she was.

I come to the conclusion that there will be more opportunities to spend time with her, especially now that I have her help with the motel.

"Ok, yeah, I can take you back." Now's definitely not the time to pry about things that are none of my business. "Are you and Nikki going to the Cedar Valley End of Summer Festival this weekend?" I ask, changing the subject.

"Nikki mentioned it, so I think we might be." She pauses and turns to me. "Are you?"

"I don't normally go." I normally don't. But I might have to break my own rules this year.

CHAPTER 17

Charlie

"Show it to me." Nikki holds her hand out for my phone.

"It's probably nothing. I changed my phone number. Maybe it's the wrong number?" I try to rationalize how he could have even obtained my number. I haven't given it to anyone back home that knows him, so it doesn't make any sense that he would have it.

"Give it to me." She shakes her hand in front of me in frustration, so I hand the phone over. I wasn't going to say anything but now that I've gotten two mysterious text messages, I need some advice.

I will find you.

"You need to go to the police." Nikki hands the phone back to me. "One text is one thing, but two with the same connotation is a different story. We don't know exactly what he's capable of."

"And what good will that do? They didn't help me before, so what is the point now? What would I even say? Oh, here's a text from an unknown number?" I don't trust the police anymore after they didn't do anything for me when he was stalking me the first time. I don't see how they can help me, anyway. The number is unknown so there isn't anything to go off of.

"The police are different here. They care. Ben knows the chief. Let him help you at least? This could very well be Alex, and you know he's resourceful. He could have dug up your number in some way that we aren't even aware exists." Nikki places her hands on my shoulders and looks me straight in the eyes. "Let Ben help."

"Ok, call him." I give in, I guess the only thing I have to lose at this point is my dignity.

"And this has happened before? Do you have those messages?" Detective Rhodes asks me in the sterile conference room of the police station.

"Not on this phone. When I came here, I got a new phone and a new number to be safe." At least, that's what I thought.

"Do you still have the old phone?" Detective Rhodes jots some notes down on his legal pad while I nervously fidget with my fingers in my lap.

"I do, it's back at the house though and dead. I would have to charge it and bring it in."

"I will run a quick trace on this phone and see if I can get any info out of it regarding that unknown number. Do you mind if I hold onto it while you run home and grab the other phone?" he asks.

I'm surprised by Detective Rhodes' willingness to do anything for me but feel grateful he's actually going to try something.

"I wouldn't stress too much right this instant," he continues. "From the sounds of these texts, this person doesn't know where you are right now, but that doesn't mean they won't find out. Be aware of your surroundings and we will work on things here."

"Thank you so much detective. I really appreciate your help. I will run home and grab the phone and drop it back off soon." Ben, Nikki, and I stand, shaking the detective's hand before leaving the conference room.

"See, I told you they would help you." Nikki wraps her arm around my shoulder as we head out of the police station.

"We will see how far they get." I sigh and get in the backseat of Ben's car. This can't be happening again. I'm finally in a town I like, with my dream business. I don't want it all to be ripped away from me.

CHAPTER 18

Charlie - past

"Why don't you come with me?" Nikki asks when she drops the bomb that she's moving to some tiny town in the middle of nowhere.

"And leave all this?" I joke, pointing around the cafe I've been working at for the last few months. I got a job here a few weeks after I escaped from Alex. I haven't seen him since I ran out that night, but he calls and texts me incessantly. I've considered blocking him or changing my number but haven't made that leap yet. I would almost rather know what he's up to seeing as how we're still in the same city. The unknown seems more frightening.

"Yes, leave all this. What are you staying for?" She finishes her sandwich sitting at the counter across from me.

"I don't hate this job. And what kind of opportunities are there in such a small town anyway?" I've always dreamed of owning my own business and the city seems like the best place to be able to do that, eventually. I don't know how I will go without seeing Nikki every day, but I do feel like I've come a long way from the girl who moved from foster home to foster home.

"A new life, that's the opportunity. You could stop looking over your shoulder constantly." She's not wrong. That's the worst part about staying in this city. However, he hasn't tracked me down yet.

"I think I will always look over my shoulder," I say, and unfortunately, I believe that. Alex always told me no one else would ever have me and I'm sure he meant it. Just because I stabbed him with a cocktail fork doesn't mean anything. That sick asshole probably got off on it after I ran out.

"You think about it. I don't leave for a couple weeks. You're more than welcome to hop in the car with me and go." She pays her tab and waves as she leaves the cafe.

I can't help but wonder what a new life would be like but too much change scares me. Change is all I have ever had in my life, and I just want some stability for once. I like my new apartment and my job, for now. Maybe someday I could go wherever Nikki said she was going. Maybe someday.

CHAPTER 19

Jude

I never go to these stupid town festivals, so I don't know why the hell I'm sitting in my truck, in the parking lot, thinking about getting out and attending this one. That's a lie. I know why.

I haven't stopped thinking about Charlie and it's driving me insane. I never get this hung up on a woman. It's killing the whole asshole vibe I like to portray. People are going to start thinking I'm getting soft.

I'm almost certain Duke was laughing at me while I was getting dressed, in his own doggo way. I never leave the house in anything but a t-shirt and jeans, so trying on every single shirt I own made my room an even bigger mess than it already was. Another clean pile of laundry on the bed for the win.

I finish off the pre-game beer I brought along, shove open the truck door with more force than I intended, and throw the empty beer can in the bed of the truck. "Fuck it, let's go," I mutter to myself under my breath.

"Boss!" I hear a voice call from the deep-fried food stand in front of me. "Boss, what the fuck are you doing here?" Rod waves me over, refusing to give up his place in line for his upcoming heart attack.

"Thought I'd check it out, nothing else to do." I shrug. I'm definitely not bringing up Charlie. Especially since he's been on Kyle about dating her.

"Sure it don't have something to do with the new dark headed girl in town?" He winks at me like he knows something. He probably does. This town has a hard time keeping secrets.

"Where's the beer tent?" I'm not having this conversation with an employee, that's for damn sure.

"Down that way boss." He points past the carnival rides that line the main street. I nod my head and turn on my heels, leaving Rod to clog his arteries on his own.

"What can I get you, honey?" The leather-skinned lady asks me from behind the table in an 'I smoke two packs a day' voice.

"A cold beer. I don't care what kind." I pause, considering my options for a moment, as she grabs a cup and heads towards a keg. "Actually, can you make that two?" The less times I have to come back over here the better.

"Sure thing." She grabs another cup, filling both to the brim with ice cold, golden beer. I toss a few bills in the tip jar after paying her, grab a cup in each hand, and turn to survey the crowd.

Sipping out of one of the cups, I spot Dane down the road at the corn hole tournament with a bunch of his buddies. Definitely not going that way. Turning to look the other way, I notice Ben, Nikki, and Charlie at the line of game stands. Bingo.

Nonchalantly, I make my way through the maze of games and farm stands to where Ben has just won Nikki a hot pink stuffed hippo. She's jumping up and down, cheering and hugging the stupid thing while Charlie smiles that fucking smile. Her eyes notice me coming up behind them and the smile fades quickly.

"Jude?" She questions, confused by my presence.

"Charlie." I take a sip out of one of the beers, holding the other out for her to take.

"I thought you don't usually come to festivals." She takes the beer out of my hand and mocks me.

I smile, which rarely happens. "I was feeling bored."

She laughs out loud, loud enough that everyone around turns and looks at us.

"Right." She sips the beer and looks up at me through those damn lashes.

"Jude, why don't you win Charlie a stuffed animal?" Nikki suggests, smiling, still holding onto her pink hippo.

"Oh, no, that's not necessary," Charlie says, shaking her head.

"Why the hell not?" I decide. I hand my beer to her and step up to the stand.

"Three balls for five dollars or ten for ten dollars," The man behind the counter says.

"Three for five." I slap down a five-dollar bill on the counter and grab three balls out of the bucket.

"Just knock down the pyramid of cups and you can win your lady prize," he says in his best carnival voice.

"Are you sure you don't need ten balls?" Charlie asks, stepping up next to me and sipping out of my beer.

"I only need one." I throw a curveball right into the pyramid of cups with enough force that they all come crashing down. Charlie's mouth drops open, as well as Nikki and Ben's.

"And that's my beer you keep drinking." I wink, reaching over and grabbing the beer out of her hand.

CHAPTER 20

Charlie

With matching pink hippos in hand, Nikki and I stand in line for the restroom while Ben and Jude wait for us by the main stage where the live band is getting ready to start.

"I still can't believe Jude knocked that pyramid down in one shot!" Nikki gushes as we move closer to the front of the line.

"Yeah, me too." I agree. It took Ben over 10 tries to finally win Nikki's stuffed animal. Jude seems to be full of surprises.

After finally being able to use the restroom, we make our way back over to Ben and Jude.

"I got you a fresh beer," Jude says, handing me a cup and smiling.

"Thank you," I reply, smiling back. I never thought Jude would show up here tonight, although, I can't say I'm upset about it. I enjoy being in his company and he's a far cry from Dane, that's for sure.

"Do you guys want to stay and watch the band, or do you want to go take a ride on the ferris wheel?" Nikki asks, finishing off the last of her drink. I look over at Jude, finding it hard to believe that he would be the ferris wheel type. He's probably not even the stand-and-listen-to-a-band type.

"Let's do the ferris wheel," he says, surprising me again.

"Are you sure?" I ask, bewildered by his behavior tonight. I mean, he's had a few beers, but I didn't think it was enough to make him go completely loopy.

"Absolutely," he says, gesturing down the street behind us. "Lead the way."

Nikki smiles and turns on her heels, looping her arm through Ben's, leading us through the crowd of people that have assembled, waiting for the band. Jude and I follow behind them, his hand resting on the small of my back as he guides me toward the spinning wheel of death. I don't hate the feel of it.

"You know," I say, looking up at him. "I didn't take you to be the ferris wheel type."

"And why's that?" he asks.

"I don't know. You just seem to not like fun very much." I shrug.

"I like fun, Charlie," he says in a barely audible voice. "I can think of a lot of fun things I would like to do with you."

I swallow hard, not exactly sure what he's referring to, but realizing that it immediately makes heat surge through my core.

<>

The carnival worker sits Nikki and Ben in their seat before moving the ferris wheel up for Jude and I to take our places. I sit down and he scoots in beside me, reaching over my lap and grabbing the buckle to strap us in. I can't tell if my nerves are coming from the fact we're on a ferris wheel, that was just assembled this morning, or if it's my close proximity to Jude.

"You seem tense," he says, throwing his hand over the back of the seat behind me and gripping my shoulder.

"I'm sorry." I grab the rail in front of us, trying not to make eye contact with him.

"Don't apologize." He squeezes my shoulder. "I'm just making sure you're okay."

I nod vigorously, "I'm good."

The carnival worker starts the ferris wheel and we begin to spin slowly towards the top.

"You know, you are kind of right," he says as we spin around on the ride.

"Oh yeah? About what?" I ask.

"About me being the ferris wheel type." He stares off into space for a moment before looking back over at me. "I just wanted to get you alone."

I can feel the heat rising in my face and I know it isn't the weather or any other outside factor making me feel the things I feel around Jude. My heart is pounding, and my palms are sweaty as the ride continues.

As much as I don't want to be feeling things for Jude, it's getting harder to deny the pull I feel toward him. I don't reply to his comment as I focus on slowing my breathing and calming my heart as the ride comes to an end and we're let out of our seat.

"Well," he says, turning towards me once we're back in the sea of people. "I need to be getting home. See you soon, Charlie." He leans down and presses a soft kiss on my forehead, then turns and walks out of sight.

CHAPTER 21

Jude

I haven't seen Charlie since the festival a couple weeks ago and have been resisting reaching out to her. I could sense how tense she was on the ferris wheel, and I don't want to come on too strong and scare her off.

Today I need to clean out the barn loft. I've been putting it off for about as long as I can at this point. You would think after all of these years it wouldn't be such a haunting task, but it is, and I hate doing it every time. I can't help the flashbacks and they hit me out of nowhere. When we were kids, Dane and I would do this together, which made it go a lot faster. Now, I would rather do it alone anyway. His company isn't something that is beneficial to me anymore.

"Duke, let's go clean out the barn." I rub him behind the ears and stand up from the table. He follows me like he always does, he's loyal to a fault. Even though fall will be here soon, the afternoon sun still heats up the barn so it's best if I get this done early.

I grab my headphones and attempt to connect them to my phone, only to realize it didn't charge last night. I plug it back in and leave it on the kitchen counter. *Dammit.* It's a lot easier when I can drown out my thoughts with music. It helps my mind not wander, but I guess today I'm just going to have to deal with it.

I slide open the door to the barn slowly with Duke right at my feet. It never fails, I always think something will be hanging from the rafters of the loft. It also never fails that I'm wrong.

Dane and I had been fishing down at the creek that morning. Mama insisted we go do something fun, and that's about all there is to do around here for fun when you're a little kid, so we packed up all of our gear and spent the morning doing just that.

We had a great day laughing and catching fish. We talked about fun times with Dad and Mama before his accident and fun things we had all done together as a family. We bonded over fishing, in the same way we bonded with our dad when he taught us how to fish.

I could tell by the location of the sun in the sky it was getting close to lunchtime, so I gathered up Dane and all of our gear and we headed back home with dirt and smiles on our faces, proud of all the fish we caught. I remember Dane asking me if we could cook the fish for dinner and being excited when I told him I would show him how to use the grill.

All in all, it was a normal day. Normal for us anyway. It had been stressful ever since Dad's accident, but we had been trying to keep things going as best we could. Somedays, Mama wouldn't even get out of bed, so I had been in charge of taking care of Dane for the most part. I made him breakfast, got him dressed for school, and walked us out to the bus.

I remember getting closer to the house and everything seemed eerily quiet. You could sense something was off. I don't know if Dane could sense it, but I definitely could.

We put all of our stuff on the porch and headed inside to have lunch, but Mama was nowhere to be found. We called and called for her, but she wasn't in the house anywhere. I told Dane to stay in the house and I headed out to check around the farm. That's when I noticed the door to the barn slightly open. I distinctly remembered shutting it after we gathered all of our fishing gear that morning.

I ran as fast as I could down to the barn but when I reached the door, I had a gut feeling that caused me to pause. I don't know if it was nerves or intuition, but I knew something was off, even at such a young age. When I slowly opened the door and saw my mother hanging from the rafters, I knew I would never be the same. I knew that day my life, and Dane's, would be changed forever.

I was too small to get her down and didn't want to untie the rope and have her fall to the ground. I screamed for her over and over, but it was too late.

Dane begged me to let him go down to the barn while we waited for the paramedics to arrive, but I refused to let him witness what I had just seen. I wouldn't put him through that. I knew I was stronger than Dane. It would have broken him.

"Jude!" I snap back to reality hearing my name being shouted from outside the barn. "Jude! Are you here?"

I drop my pitchfork and run out of the barn to see Charlie rushing towards me from her car parked in the driveway.

"It's Hazel!"

CHAPTER 22

Charlie

Instead of driving my own car back to Hazel's, I jump in Jude's truck with him. "She asked me to come get you and refused to let me call 9-1-1. I'm so sorry."

We fly down the gravel road at a very unsafe speed and I hold onto the handle above my head as tight as I can.

"She said she fell trying to grab something out of one of her upper cabinets," I say in a rush. "But she couldn't reach her phone to call you herself. I tried calling you, but you didn't answer, that's why I drove."

"Stop explaining yourself. It's okay," he says as he runs his hand through his hair. "This is just how Hazel is. She's going to put up a fight to go to the hospital. She thinks she's invincible. This isn't my first rodeo."

"Whatever you need, I'm here. I'm just glad I came out here today or who knows how long she would have laid there," I say and I notice him flinch at my words.

We pull up to Hazel's house and Jude throws the truck into park, both of us rushing out of the vehicle to get inside as quickly as possible.

"I'm back Hazel. I have Jude," I announce as I fling open the screen door to the house, almost hitting Jude right in the face.

"Hazel, what happened?" Jude rushes to her side and kneels on the kitchen floor next to her.

"I'll be fine honey, if you could just get me up and to my bed." Hazel tries to sit by herself but can't. "It's just a banged-up leg, I'll be fine."

"That's not going to happen, Hazel. Charlie and I are going to get you up, but then we're taking you to the hospital and I don't want to hear any arguments about it." Jude motions for me to come help him. I lean down on the other side of Hazel and wrap my arm through hers as Jude and I proceed to help her up.

"Jude, you always take such good care of ol' Hazel." She smiles as we lift her off the kitchen floor. "I really think I will be just fine after some rest."

"You think so, Hazel?" I laugh at her remark. "Try putting weight on your leg." I wink at Jude, knowing she's not going to be able to. She tries and winces looking back and forth between Jude and I, knowing the inevitable.

"See, Hazel. We can't leave you here alone if you can't even walk. Charlie and I are going to get you out to the truck and then we will go to the hospital to get this leg checked out. It's better to be safe than sorry and it will make me feel better. Do it for me?" he pleads with her.

"Fine." She winces and we move out of the house, down the porch and into the truck. It makes my heart swell with warmth when I watch him care for Hazel. He has such compassion for her.

I wonder if he would be that compassionate with me or if he would turn into a monster like so many other men I know have. I find it hard to believe that he and Dane came from the same set of parents.

The ride to the hospital is quick as Jude races into town. We would have still been waiting at the house for paramedics, so this was definitely a better idea. We pull up to the emergency room entrance and Jude rushes inside, quickly coming back out with a nurse and a wheelchair.

Hazel huffs in the truck as I open her door. "I don't need a wheelchair."

"Don't argue, Hazel." Jude scolds her and helps her out of the truck and into the chair. She sulks as the nurse pushes her into the hospital. Jude and I follow behind them as the nurse checks Hazel in and takes her back to a room.

"I'm just going to take some vitals and the doctor will be in soon," the nurse says with a smile as she places the blood pressure cuff around Hazel's arm. "I would bet he's going to want to do an x-ray, if not an MRI, so that we can get a good picture of what's happening inside there."

"She's probably not going to be a very good patient, so I hope you and the doc can handle her." Jude shoots a glaring look at Hazel as if he's warning her to be good.

"I'll be good." Hazel frowns and the tone in her voice doesn't make me believe she's telling the truth. I laugh internally. These doctors have no idea what they are in for.

The door to the room opens and a tall, middle-aged man in a white coat walks in. "Hello, Hazel. I'm Doctor Williams. What brings you in today?"

"She fell trying to reach something in a high cabinet in her kitchen," I say, answering for Hazel knowing she's not going to tell the doctor the whole story. "I found her lying on the floor when I stopped by earlier. I'm not sure how long she was lying there, but we got her here as soon as we could."

"Ah, well, we should probably get an x-ray at least and then go from there. I will have the nurse take you down to radiology. If you two want to have a seat in the waiting room, we will come find you when we have some answers." The doctor stands and shakes both of our hands before exiting the room.

"We will be in the waiting room, Hazel. Go easy on them, eh? They are just trying to take care of you." Jude gives her a kiss on the forehead, and I pat her hand, following him out of the room.

It only took a couple hours before we had the results from Hazel's tests. She ended up with a dislocated hip, fortunately, not broken. The doctor, however, was concerned about some results that came back with her bloodwork. He said it suggested she was prone to blood clots and that this injury could exacerbate it. He's prescribing her blood thinners and stressed the importance of her taking them.

When the doctor leaves us in the waiting room, Jude turns to me and sighs. "Well, your car is back at my house and it's dinner time. Let me take you to get something to eat before we head back out of town?"

"You don't have to do that, Jude. I can scrounge up something at home. You look exhausted." I don't want to burden him, and I'm sure he's tired after such a long day.

"Charlie, you aren't an inconvenience, ever. I'm starving, and unlike you, I don't have anything to 'scrounge up' at home." He makes air quotes with his finger when he says 'scrounge up' and grins as we walk out of the hospital toward his truck. "*Let me* take you to dinner."

"Fine." I laugh. Yeah, he doesn't look like the type that spends a lot of time grocery shopping.

CHAPTER 23

Jude

"Thank you for everything today. It really means so much to me that you care for Hazel, she's like a grandmother to me." I take a long sip of my beer. "Mmm yep, I needed this."

"You don't need to thank me. I do care for Hazel and there's nowhere I would have rather been today." She takes a sip of her own beer and smiles at me across the table. I still feel torn about the things that smile makes me feel deep inside my chest.

"Are you sure about that? I could probably think of at least ten places I would have rather been today than at the hospital." She laughs at my comment. I can't help but notice again how beautiful she is. I don't think I could ever tire of hearing her laugh or seeing how her eyes light up when she smiles. It's a little unnerving how she makes me feel.

I've pretty much closed myself off since everything happened with Katie.

"Okay, maybe it wasn't the ideal day but I'm really happy I could be there for you…and Hazel, of course." She stutters and looks away quickly like she regrets what she said.

"Yeah, I know what you mean." She enjoyed being with me today. It's been a long while since I have spent time with a woman I actually wanted to be around, and someone who wanted to be around me for something other than my dick.

I shouldn't be nervous, but I do feel some anxiety sitting here alone with her. It's like every sense in my body is heightened when she's around. I don't want to say anything stupid or mess anything up. We sit in silence for what seems like a lifetime before she finally speaks again.

"Oh, I love this song!" She smiles across the table at me as a familiar song plays through the bar. "Dance with me?"

I frown at her, "I don't dance."

"Oh, come on, Jude. Just once, let loose a little." She wiggles back and forth in her seat, and I immediately imagine her doing that, on my lap. *Fuck.* "Are you embarrassed that you can't dance?"

I chug the last of my beer and set it on the table. Standing, I stretch my hand out to grab hers. She places her hand in mine, and we move out to the middle of the floor where there are a few other couples already dancing.

I wrap my arm around her waist, pull her close enough our bodies are touching and begin swaying back and forth to the music.

"Oh…" She trails off, surprised by the sudden movement.

"I never said I couldn't dance." I lean in close and whisper against the soft skin behind her ear. "I said I *don't* dance." She places her hand around the back of my neck and begins twirling her fingers in my hair.

I haven't had a woman touch me like this in a long time. I've forgotten how it feels and hope that she can't feel the fast pace of my heartbeat, or my growing erection. I try to put some space between us but she's not letting go.

I can't help but start to acknowledge how good she feels wrapped around me. Too good. This is probably a mistake, and I will probably regret it tomorrow. This damn bar always has that effect on me.

We sway back and forth for the entirety of the song, and it seems like everything else around us has disappeared. It's only her and I, unsure of what's happening between us, but neither of us questioning it out loud. When the song finally ends, I find myself wishing it would have played a little bit longer.

"Not bad." She smiles as we head back to our table. "Another beer?" she asks as we sit down.

"Absolutely." I grin back at her and waste no time flagging down our waitress. I'm going to need more than a couple tonight. I don't know what kind of spell this woman is trying to put me under but I'm not sure I can deal with it completely sober.

"So, tell me something about you that no one else knows," I ask, challenging her to open up. I want to know everything there is to know about her.

"Hmmm..." She ponders and takes another long sip of her beer. "That might be kind of hard. Nikki knows pretty much everything about me."

"Best friends don't count." I'm not letting her get out of this question.

"Okay." She sits silently for a moment, trying to think of something to say until she finally comes up with, "I don't like ferris wheels."

I laugh, sensing she's uncomfortable with deep conversations. "Then why on earth did we go on one?" I take another long pull off my beer. Maybe that's why she seemed so tense that night.

"Honestly?" she asks.

"Of course." I respond.

"I also wanted to be alone with you." She looks at me nervously.

"I see." I nod, realizing the nerves I was sensing could have been from me as well. "Tell me something else."

"Um, well, I have really bad luck with relationships." She shrugs and looks down at the table. "I mean, every single one I have ever been in ends badly. So, it's either me or there aren't any good ones left."

"Don't be embarrassed. I have a similar past with relationships." I reach across the table and grab her hand, hoping she can feel that I can relate to her. She gives me a shy smile in return.

"Tell me? I can't imagine grumpy, private Jude having trouble with women." She raises her brow, and her eyes do that *lighting up* thing again. I can't help but indulge her.

"I was in a pretty serious relationship a while back. I honestly thought I was going to spend the rest of my life with her. Things were going really well…" I pause, reluctant, but continue anyway, "well, until they weren't. She started getting really distant with me and I knew something was up. Then one night, I caught her with… someone else… and that was it for me. I was done."

"Wow. I'm so sorry that happened to you." She traces her finger along the rim of her glass. "Something similar happened to me recently too, so I understand all of the mental stuff that comes along with that. All the questions and self-doubt."

I nod, agreeing. "And I'm sorry that happened to you, as well." I can't imagine someone cheating on Charlie. If she was mine, there's no way I would let her go.

After dinner, we drove back to my farm to get Charlie's car. "I'm sorry we stayed out so late." I apologize as I park the truck.

"Oh, don't apologize, Jude. I actually had a wonderful time tonight. It's been a long time since…" She doesn't finish her sentence and turns her head to stare out the window.

"Yeah, it has." I agree. I know what she means. She doesn't have to say it. She opens her door to exit the truck and I follow her lead. I'm not sure what the right thing to do here is. I haven't been able to stop thinking about how her lips felt on mine since I kissed her in the bar a couple weeks ago. I follow her to her car. She turns to face me once she reaches the driver's side.

"Jude, thank you, really, I needed tonight more than I realized." She tucks her hair behind her ear, looks up at me through her lashes and I can't help myself. I move closer to her, placing my hands against her car on each side of her, pinning her against the door.

"Oh…" She gasps at the closeness and her lips part ever so slightly making me smile. "Jude."

"Charlotte," I respond, looking down at her. She really is the most beautiful thing I've ever laid eyes on.

"Charlie," She corrects.

"Charlie…" I sigh. "I'm having a really difficult time controlling myself around you. If you keep torturing me, I'm not going to be able to continue to resist you." I lean in closer, pinning her against the car harder than before. "I haven't stopped thinking about you since that night at O'Henry's a couple weeks ago." I pause, running my thumb across her lips. "Actually, that's a lie. I haven't stopped thinking about you since the farmer's market."

"You haven't?" she asks, as if it's the most ridiculous thing she's ever heard someone say to her. "And I'm not torturing you on purpose. I don't know what you mean."

"The way you look at me through your lashes, your laugh, your smile. It's all torture. As much as I want to stop thinking about you, I can't. It's impossible."

"You don't want to think about me?" She leans farther back into the car to look me in the eyes better, placing her hands on my chest.

"I don't want to hurt you…and…well, I'm afraid I will." I've never been this honest with anyone before, but she deserves the truth. I'm damaged goods and there's no way this will end well for either of us.

"I don't think that's possible, Jude. Now, are you going to kiss me or not? Because if you aren't…I…"

I don't give her time to finish talking. In one quick movement I grab the back of her neck and slam my mouth against hers, parting her lips with mine, searching for her tongue. She tastes so sweet, and her lips are like heaven. She kisses me back with the same amount of need and I can feel the fire burning between us. She grabs the back of my neck and I move my hands down, gripping her waist. I should stop this before it goes any further, but my judgment is clouded.

As if reading each other's minds, she jumps at the same time I lift and she wraps her legs around my waist, pressing herself into me. We both fall back into the side of the car, our mouths never leaving each other in the process.

I pause for a moment and pull back, searching her eyes, for what, I'm not sure. She glances toward the house, and I don't think twice. I push us off the car and begin kissing her again, this time walking towards the house with her legs still wrapped around my waist. I'm certain she can feel how hard I'm with how tightly she's wrapped around me, but I decide that I don't care. I try not to stumble as I make my way up the stairs of the porch.

I turn the knob with one hand still under her ass and kick open the door with my foot. As we enter the house she begins tugging at my shirt, trying to get it over my head. We pause against the entryway wall, and I help her lift it over my head. I turn around, pushing her back up against the wall, pinning her there with my body.

I remove her shirt and toss it to the ground. "You're stunning." I say running my hands up her sides and flicking one of her hard nipples beneath my thumb. A small moan escapes her parted lips as she tilts her head back against the wall and arches her back. I find the small space I'm looking for on her neck and bite down softly before trailing kisses down to her chest. Her fingers tighten in my hair, sending shivers down my spine.

"Bedroom?" she whispers into my ear. I don't need to be asked twice. I shouldn't be doing this, but I'm tired of controlling myself.

Once we finally get to the bedroom, I toss her down onto the bed. Slowly moving up her body, my hands reach the waistband of her jeans. She quickly puts her hands on mine. "Jude, wait." she says, hesitating.

I look up at her. "Is everything okay?" She looks like she wants to say something but just smiles and nods her head. I get back to work, unbuttoning her jeans and sliding them, along with her black underwear, down her legs. I toss them on the floor next to the bed and make my way back in between her legs. I run my hand up her thigh and slip two fingers into her. "So wet."

"Mmmm." She moans pushing her hips into my hand. I slip my fingers out and lick them while she watches me intently, her blue eyes darker than usual.

"So sweet." I place my fingers back inside her sliding them in and out while circling her clit with my tongue.

"Jude…" she breathes. I love the sound of my name coming out of her mouth while I'm devouring her. I could get used to this. She continues to move underneath me as I torture her with my tongue.

"I'm going to come," she says, breathless.

"Come for me then, baby. Don't hold back." I continue circling her clit with my tongue and sliding my fingers out, picking up the pace when I start feeling her pulse around them. Watching her grab the sheets in her fists, arch her back and come undone because of me is the most amazing sight I have ever seen.

"Fuck me," she breathes once she's able to speak again. I move up her body and kiss her as she unbuttons my jeans and slides them down my legs with her foot.

"Nice trick." I smile kicking my jeans onto the floor. She smiles back, playing with the hair on the back of my head with one hand and kissing me again, moving her other hand and sliding it down my side, finally finding my hard cock and grabbing it. She slicks the precum over the tip, driving me crazy in the process.

A groan escapes my throat and I line myself up to the entrance of her sweet pussy and slide in slowly, her back arching and a moan escaping her lips at the same time.

"You're so fucking amazing," I whisper into her ear as I kiss down her neck. She wraps her legs around my waist and meets each of my thrusts with her own. We keep the same pace for as long as I can stand, her teeth sinking into my skin.

"I'm not going to last very long if you keep biting my neck like that." A groan escapes me as she bites down harder. I can tell she's smiling at the power she has over me right now.

"What are you waiting for then, come for me *baby*." She mimics my tone from earlier and continues biting my neck. Those simple words send me over the edge as my own orgasm courses through my body. Once I catch my breath, I move to the side to lay next to her in bed.

"Stay with me." I run my hand down her side as we lie facing each other in bed. "It's late."

"I don't know." She furrows her brows.

"I want you to stay. I told you I don't say things I don't mean." I haven't slept with a woman in a long time, but this feels right, and I honestly don't want her driving back to town in the middle of the night. Plus, a warm body next to me wouldn't hurt either.

"Okay," she concedes.

CHAPTER 24

Charlie

Nikki is covering the store for me so I can run a couple errands today. She had quite a few questions about where I was last night, and I promised I would tell her everything when I returned. Plus, I need time to process everything that happened. I shouldn't be jumping into bed with Jude. I hardly even know him, and the last time that happened, I ended up with Alex, and that ended with a cocktail fork sticking out of his leg.

I can't deny there's something different about Jude. When I'm with him I don't get that nasty feeling in the pit of my stomach. He has kind eyes and that's not hard to notice. But, what if I'm too messed up for someone like Jude? What if once he finds out about my past, he decides

I'm too much trouble? I'm not sure I could handle losing the one man in my life that actually seems to care about me.

When I was checking out at the grocery store with new items for our coffee bar at the store, my phone started to ring. Detective Rhodes' name showed on the screen, and I answered, nervous of what news he had to share.

"Hello?" I answer, reluctantly.

"Miss Collins. Would you have some time to stop by the station?" he responds without pleasantries.

"I'm at the store right now. I could be there in ten minutes or so." I fumble the coffee pods I was attempting to grab from the shelf, and they crash to the floor, breaking open and spilling all over the aisle. *Shit.*

"Perfect, I will be here," he says, hanging up before I can ask anything else.

I gather up all of the coffee pods that are strewn throughout the aisle and try not to make eye contact with the other shoppers staring at me. I'm feeling anxious enough already.

A little more than ten minutes later, I pull into the parking lot and see Detective Rhodes outside on the phone. "Good morning, Detective," I say as I reach the door and he ends his call.

"Good morning, Miss Collins. Join me inside?" He opens the door for me and follows me into the station. "To the left down the hall, we can talk in my office."

I sit across from him at his desk. His office is quite opposite of the sterile conference room I was in the first time we were here. His desk is a warm, dark wood and photos of his family, I assume, adorn the walls which are painted a soft taupe.

I'm nervous to speak as I take in the room, and he grabs a stack of papers from a file folder. I hope he has good news for me.

"When we traced the text from your current cell phone the other day, we only got a location, not a name. In searching through your old phone and tracing those threatening texts, we found something interesting. See here…" He turns the document in front of him toward me and points to a series of numbers.

I take a minute to study the information in front of me. "I'm sorry, Detective, what am I looking at here? Most of these numbers are exactly the same." He's going to have to spell it out for me.

"Precisely. These are the IP addresses of the locations where the text messages sent to you are coming from. These on the left are from the old phone and these on the right are from your new phone. They are the same. This confirms, at least in my belief, that we do have some cause for concern here." Detective Rhodes leans back in his chair and waits for me to process what he has just told me.

"So, Alex is sending these messages to me?" I feel my face redden and sweat bead up on my forehead. This is my worst nightmare.

"I do believe that is the case, although I don't have that one hundred percent confirmed at this time. I have a call into the law enforcement agency that handles the jurisdiction of this IP address. I hope to hear back from them today, tomorrow at the latest. Until then, and going forward, keep your wits about you Miss Collins. If anything else suspicious happens, please let me know right away." He slides a business card towards me. "I wrote my personal cell phone here for you. Please call that number."

"Thank you for everything, Detective. I greatly appreciate all the work you are putting into this for me."

I leave the station, frazzled and even more anxious with this new information Detective Rhodes just dropped on me. I try to focus and gather myself before arriving at the hospital. I'm hoping Hazel is feeling better today than she was when Jude and I left last night. I pull into the parking lot of the hospital and find a spot quickly. I told Nikki I would only be gone an hour or two and I don't want to disturb Hazel for too long. She needs her rest.

As I make my way into the hospital, I can't help but keep thinking about everything that happened with Jude last night. I'm so torn and hope that we didn't make a mistake. I care for Jude and he's a wonderful friend, but I would be lying to myself if I said I'm not developing feelings for him. I haven't laughed or connected with someone on that level in probably my entire life, besides Nikki I suppose. What a mess. I have to find time to tell him about Dane. I can't continue this without him knowing.

I reach the end of the hallway and knock quietly on Hazel's door. I can hear her talking inside, so I slowly push it open and peek around it, expecting to see Jude.

Hazel is lying in bed and there is a man in the chair next to her facing away from me. It's definitely not Jude and from the back I would almost say it looks like… "Dane?" *Did I just say that out loud?*

His head swings around and he looks like he's seen a ghost. His face goes pale, and he stands quickly, smoothing his shirt nervously.

"Charlie?" He sounds confused and unsure of why I'm here.

"Do you two know each other?" I hear Hazel ask from behind him. *Unfortunately.* I can't believe he's here. She said she hadn't seen him in years when we spoke about him last. I mean, I guess he has every right to be here but of course, it's my fucking luck he's here. Right now. When I am.

"I was just leaving." He turns to Hazel and grabs her hand. "It was good to see you, Hazel. I'll stop back by tomorrow and check on you."

"Thanks for coming by." She smiles at him as he lets go of her hand and rushes past me to get out the door as fast as he can.

"Hello, dear," she says, turning to face me. "I'm glad you stopped." She looks past me to the door. "What was that all about?"

"Oh…it's nothing. Don't you worry about it. How are you feeling?" I take the seat next to her that was occupied by the asshole just a few minutes before.

"Don't worry about old Hazel. The doctor said I should be able to go home in a couple weeks as long as my leg heals up good. So, there's no need to fret. I'll be out of here in no time."

"I'm glad to hear that." I smile, patting the top of her hand and looking back over my shoulder out of instinct.

"Dear…please tell Hazel what's wrong. How do you and Dane know each other?"

"I'm afraid I have gotten myself into quite a mess, Hazel. Do you promise you won't say a word to Jude? I know how he feels about Dane, and I don't want to cause more trouble. I would prefer to tell him myself." Causing even more problems between Jude and Dane is the last thing I want, even if I do fear it may be too late for that.

"I promise dear. You have my word." She holds out her pinky for me and I wrap mine around hers, smiling.

"I was seeing Dane the first few months after I moved here. It wasn't serious or anything, but I caught him with his assistant on his birthday. I didn't know he and Jude were brothers. He actually told me he didn't have any family. I broke it off with him as soon as I caught him. But…" I hesitate, weary of what I'm about to share with Hazel. "I spent last night with Jude. It wasn't planned, it just happened. And now, well, now I'm not sure what to do." I sigh, letting my shoulders relax more. Hazel is so easy to talk to. Much like Jude. I wonder if that's where he gets it from.

"Katie?" Hazel questions.

"You know Katie?" My eyebrows shoot up at the name coming out of her mouth.

"I've heard of her." She looks out the window for a minute and then turns back to me. I should have known Hazel would know Katie. Hazel knows everything about everyone in this town. "Dane and Jude are two different people. Dane has always been a little less…trustworthy… I guess that is the best word. They both struggled after their parents died and Jude just matured a lot faster, although he didn't really have a choice. That doesn't excuse Dane's behavior, of course, but it does show you the type of man Jude is. He wouldn't hurt a fly…on purpose at least." She smiles and I know she's right. "As far as you spending the night with Jude, I think that is wonderful, dear. Jude is kind and caring. He's guarded because he's been hurt in the past, but I had a feeling you would be able to bring him out of his shell."

"I think Jude is a very great friend and I'm glad to have met both of you. I just feel uncomfortable around Dane, and I have to figure out how to tell Jude before things get out of hand." It seems as though I might be seeing more of Dane if he's going to reconnect with Hazel, in which case I guess I'll just have to suck it up and deal with it.

CHAPTER 25

Jude

Waking up with Charlie in bed next to me was more than I could have hoped for. She's so different from any other woman I've met. I feel like I can relate to her on a different level with both of our past relationship experiences. There's still a nagging thought in the back of my head telling me that I shouldn't get deeply involved with her, and I can only attribute that to the fact I'm sometimes so messed up in the head that I worry I will damage her in the process of figuring out myself.

She didn't stay long this morning, saying she had errands to run. I would have kept her in bed much longer, but I didn't want to come on too strong after one night together. This pull between right and wrong inside my head is going to be the death of me.

After Charlie left, I made coffee and took Duke out back to throw the ball for him before I had to run to the jobsite. Since firing Kyle, I've had to be more present for the guys in making sure everything is getting accomplished on time. Fucking Kyle. I really could have used him on this job, but I don't fuck around with guys who charge at women. That's not the kind of employee I want representing my business.

Duke runs back from the yard, tennis ball and slobber in tow. "Good boy, Duke." I scratch him on the head and grab the ball out of his mouth. "What do you think of Charlie?" I ask him like he's going to respond to me. Maybe I do need a woman in my life, I seem to only have real conversations with a dog.

He nods his head and even though I'm sure he just wants me to throw his ball, I'm going to take it as he's saying he likes her.

On my way into town, I stop over at Hazel's when I see a car I've never seen before in the driveway. Pulling in, I see the man leaving a notice in her screen door. I park the truck as he turns to come down the steps.

"What can I help you with, sir?" I ask, walking toward the man who is clearly out of his element. He's wearing a button-down shirt, tie, and slacks. Not something you see out on a farm.

"I'm looking for Hazel Petersen." The man straightens his tie. "Doesn't appear she's home though."

"I'm her grandson, what can I help you with?" This man looks like trouble, and I don't like the air of arrogance that is wafting off him.

"Oh, um, I've been trying to get ahold of her about her tax payment, but she hasn't been returning my calls. If we don't have it by the end of the month, we're going to have to take control of the property."

"I see. Well, don't worry, we will have that taken care of by then. You can be on your way now." These assholes only care about money and I'm so tired of them threatening to take away farmland from people who have been in this community for generations.

I'm going to have to pay a visit to the one person I don't want to. *Fuck.*

CHAPTER 26

Charlie

Nikki suggested grabbing drinks after we closed the bookstore, and I honestly couldn't think of anything better to do. I was still reeling from everything Detective Rhodes told me and everything that happened with Jude last night, so I knew distracting myself with dinner and drinks would at least keep my mind occupied.

"It sounds like Detective Rhodes has everything under control, so now spill it. Where the hell were you last night." Nikki muses as she sips her beer.

"I…well…I…it's a long story." I stumble over my words. I don't even know how to start this conversation.

"You didn't come home…and you know no one in this town. Except…" She wiggles her eyebrows at me, already knowing what happened even though I haven't said a word.

"I know. This is terrible!" I shriek, throwing one hand in the air while chugging my beer with the other. "I'm so fucked. With everything that is going on with Alex, the texts, Dane and now this."

"You are not fucked. This is good. Yeah, the other stuff sucks, but this…this part is good. Tell me, was it as amazing as I imagine it was?" Her voice is full of curiosity, and I can't deny that it was amazing.

I lower my shoulders and plant my face in my palm, "I don't even have words to describe it." I surrender. There's nothing more, or less, that I can do. "What a mess I've gotten myself into."

"It's not a mess, it's just a hurdle. I'm going to assume you haven't told Jude about Dane?" she asks, finishing off her first beer.

"I was going to but didn't want to ruin the moment. I can't let this go any further without telling him. I have to make sure he hears it from me." It would be terrible if he heard it from someone else. He would be so hurt and probably never speak to me again.

"I think you should do it sooner rather than later. You definitely don't want him hearing it from someone else, I agree with that. Are you going to tell him about the texts?" Nikki motions for the bartender. "Can we get two more? And why don't you just keep them coming?"

"Are you trying to get me drunk again?" I ask, raising my brow at her. "And no, I don't plan on bringing him into that mess." At the sound of the bell over the door, I turn around.

"Oh no."

CHAPTER 27

Jude

My visit with Dane went better than I expected but damn, I need a drink now. We haven't spoken in five years, but I really need his help right now and had hoped he would understand the gravity of the situation Hazel was facing.

I decided not to call him, mainly because I wasn't sure he even had the same cell phone number, but also because I didn't want to give him the chance to refuse to see me.

I arrived at his office and sat in my truck for quite a while before deciding to just rip off the band aid. I knew Katie would be inside and I would have to face her as well.

Just as I suspected, she was sitting behind her desk filling out some paperwork when I walked in.

"Jude." She was startled to see me, and I wasn't surprised seeing as how the last time we spoke it was less than cordial.

She dropped her pen and fumbled with the papers nervously as I walked up to her desk. "What…what can I help you with?

"I need to see Dane." I'm not going to make small talk; this is purely business.

"Um…okay…I think he just got out of a meeting. One sec." She heads down the hallway to his office. I can hear them talking quietly and I pace around the lobby. She comes back out after a few minutes, "You can go back.".

I walk down the hall and find him sitting behind his desk, refusing to look up at me. I knock on the door jam and let myself in.

"Have a seat, Jude," I say sarcastically to myself, as I sit down.

"What do you want?" he asks, eyes not looking up from his phone.

"Well, first, eye contact. Quit being a pussy. I wouldn't be here if this wasn't important." I'm not going to deal with his victim bullshit when he's the one who has caused all these problems.

He snaps his head up, sets his phone down and leans back in his chair, waiting for me to speak.

"It's Hazel."

"I've already been to see Hazel." He looks at me accusingly and I can't help but feel anger boiling up inside me. I don't know where he gets off thinking he has any right to know anything regarding Hazel, except for what I'm about to tell him.

"You went to see Hazel in the hospital?" I'm honestly shocked he made any sort of effort.

"I did." He's unmoving, challenging me like he knows what I'm here for.

"That's not why I'm here."

"Then why are you here?" God, this is so much fun. Why can't he grow the fuck up and act like a man?

"She's going to lose the farm." That gets his attention. He sits up straighter in his chair now, leaning forward on his desk.

"What do you mean?" He's interested now. Good.

"She hasn't made the tax payment. They told me if she doesn't pay it by the end of the month, they are taking the farm from her. I have half the payment, and I think after everything Hazel has done for you, you should come up with the other half. It's the least you can do for all the trouble and hurt you've caused her."

He sits still for a while, pondering my demand. If he refuses, I will get it out of him anyway. He's done nothing but cause that woman heartbreak since he came back to town.

"How much?" he finally asks.

"Thirty-five hundred dollars." At least he's asking how much. That's a start.

"So, you don't have the decency to tell me that Hazel was hospitalized, but you have the nerve to come asking me for money?" Ah, yes, there it is. I was wondering when the true Dane would surface.

"If you aren't willing to come up with the other half, then you aren't allowed to see Hazel again. You can't keep breaking her heart. It will kill her." He ponders my words for a bit before opening his top desk drawer and pulling out a checkbook.

CHAPTER 28

Charlie

"What?" Nikki turns around quickly. "Shit." She turns back to look at me and I'm sure all the blood has drained from my face.

"Please don't come over here…please don't." I whisper under my breath hiding my face with my hand.

"Charlie, can we talk?" Dane asks from behind where we're seated at the bar.

"She's not interested, you've done enough." Nikki snaps, answering for me.

"It's fine, Nikki." Turning my attention to Dane and grabbing my beer, "Let's get this over with." I hop off my barstool and motion to a booth towards the back of the bar. He takes the lead and I follow, sliding into the booth across from him.

"What do you want?" I ask, taking a long sip of my beer and shooting daggers at him through my eyes.

"I just want to say I'm sorry. I know I screwed up and I just wanted to say that. That's all."

"Listen, Dane. It's fine, really. There's no need to even feel bad about it. I'm thankful, honestly. You showed me that you aren't someone I want to waste my time with and I'm grateful I found out before things got more serious. So, don't waste your time wallowing in it. Move on."

"Have you?" he asks. Like he has a right to know what's going on in my life. What an asshole. It's so crazy how different he is from Jude.

"It's none of your business." I want nothing more than to end this conversation, so I begin to scoot myself out of the booth when the bell on the bar door rings again and I see Jude step in. I don't even notice the smile that forms on my lips but clearly Dane doesn't miss it. He looks back and forth between Jude and I. The next thing I know, he's on his feet.

"You've got to be fucking kidding me." His mouth falls open as Jude notices us in the back corner. I would have thought Jude saw a ghost by the look on his face seeing Dane and I together. *Fuck*. This isn't how this was supposed to go. His gaze goes cold, and he immediately turns and walks back out the door, slamming it shut behind him.

"*Him?*" Dane looks at me like I owe him an explanation. I don't say a word and run towards the door after Jude.

"Charlie!" I hear Nikki shout from the bar as I dart out the door, looking in both directions for a sign of Jude. I see him round the corner towards the side of the bar.

"Jude! Wait!" I yell after him, following him around the side of the bar. I see him opening the door to get into his truck. "Jude!" He turns on his heels causing me to stop.

"Not now." He states, moving closer and stopping a few feet in front of me. "Not… now." He repeats.

"Please, let me explain." I beg. "It's not what you think." Fuck, I've really messed this up. I should have told him last night when I had the chance. He puts his hands up as if to insinuate he doesn't want me to come closer. Instead of continuing towards him I stop, and my shoulders slump out of instinct. "Okay." It's all I can muster at this point. If there's one thing I know about Jude, it's that this conversation is going to go nowhere tonight. I look back up at him, defeated.

"This," he points his finger back and forth between us both, "was a mistake."

I don't know how to respond to him. I just stare back and feel the tears burning the back of my eyes. After the day I had and now this, I can't help but feel emotional. I tell myself I will not cry. I will not. I will myself to just turn around and walk away but my feet won't move, and I feel a lone tear fall down my cheek. I drop my head hoping he doesn't notice. I nod, shifting on my feet and fiddling with my fingers as my anxiety gets the best of me.

"I'm sorry you feel that way." I'm surprised at how much this hurts right now. I barely know Jude and my feelings shouldn't be this strong at this point, but it appears my heart has different plans than my head does. He opens his mouth to speak but instead turns around, gets in his truck and speeds out of the parking lot.

CHAPTER 29

Charlie - past

Alex wasn't letting up with his incessant texting. If anything, it had gotten worse. I was receiving at least twenty text messages per day and my phone was ringing off the hook. The police weren't interested in helping me, so I decided to help myself. He still must not know where I live because, if he did, I'm sure he would have been here by now. Tonight is Nikki's going away party at her apartment and even though I'm sad for my best friend to leave, I'm happy that she's found Ben. He's great for her. I can only hope to find someone like him someday.

"I'm going to miss you so much!" Nikki squeals as she hugs me.

"Me too. Maybe I can come visit once you are settled in." We enjoy our last evening together in the same city reminiscing about when we were kids and our hopes for the future. I know it's not goodbye forever, but goodbye's still sting anyway.

"Are you sure you don't want to go? I still have room for you in the car." She's been insistent about convincing me to go with her, but I just can't leave yet.

"I really do appreciate the offer, but I just can't." I feel bad but I've got a lead on a new business venture I'm working on and it's an opportunity I hate to pass up. "I have a meeting next week with the Chamber of Commerce about opening a store. I have to see that through. You know it's my dream."

"I know. I'm just sad I won't be able to experience it with you." She uncorks another bottle of champagne and fills our glasses. Raising them together she toasts, "To best friends and new beginnings."

"To best friends and new beginnings," I repeat, unsure about what lies ahead for both of us.

CHAPTER 30

Jude

I feel terrible about how I left things with Charlie last night, but I cannot continue to be a fool about stuff like this when it comes to Dane. I already know what he's capable of doing and I refuse to let myself get caught up in any of his messes again. I don't think my heart can take another woman leaving me for him.

After I finish the chores at my place, I head over to Hazel's to complete hers. She'll be able to come home soon but I need to make sure things don't get behind while she's in the hospital. I promised I would visit again today so once I'm done here, I plan to head into town to see her and then check on the motel.

I can't help but think about Charlie and her words to me last night. She said it wasn't what it looked like, but I've heard that before. Katie said the same thing when I caught her with Dane. It's not something I would have expected, and then again, I never expected it out of Katie either. Of course, I expect behavior like that out of Dane. It's who he is and clearly, he isn't changing. Hazel knows about all of that, so maybe I can have a talk with her if she's feeling up to it. I don't want to stress her or hinder her progress, but she's the only person I can really count on anymore.

I finish feeding the goats at Hazel's and head into town. It's a beautiful fall day and the leaves are turning, signaling winter will be here before we know it. I'm not ready for the cold weather but each season is important, and I've learned to embrace it as I get older.

The hospital is quieter today. The halls are emptier than the past couple times I have visited. I reach Hazel's room and the door is cracked open just a bit. I raise my hand to knock on the door but pause. I can hear talking inside, so I lean in closer to listen.

"Oh dear, I know you were hoping to tell him yourself. He will come around. Just give him some time." I hear Hazel say. I shouldn't be eavesdropping, but my curiosity gets the better of me.

I hear a familiar voice respond. "I've really made a mess out of all this. I don't know what I'm doing anymore, Hazel. Thanks for the talk though, I really needed it." *Shit*, it's Charlie.

I immediately walk down the hallway, around the corner, and find the men's restroom. I don't want to listen in on that conversation. I definitely don't want to run into Charlie today. I'll give it a few minutes and see if she's gone. But, dammit, her voice shouldn't make me feel the things I'm feeling. Especially after last night. I stare at myself in the mirror and splash some water on my face. *Get it together, Jude.*

I wait five minutes and make my way out of the restroom, peeking around the corner. I don't see Charlie, so I slowly move towards Hazel's room. I don't hear voices anymore, so I open the door and see Hazel in her room, alone. *Phew.*

"Hazel. You're looking better today." I smile, walking in and taking the seat next to her bed.

"Oh, if it isn't Mr. Assumptions." She looks at me coldly and turns her head back towards the window, attempting to ignore me.

"I'm sorry?" What in the world has Charlie done to turn Hazel against me?

"Oh, don't act so shocked. You just missed Charlie. She filled me in on what you did last night." She looks at me accusingly and I can't help but feel angry that Charlie has pretty much tattled on me when I didn't do anything wrong. What are we, twelve?

"What *I* did? What are you talking about? I caught her with Dane at O'Henry's last night. Did she tell you that part? I would think you of all people would understand, Hazel." She knows very well what happened with Dane and Katie so I cannot believe what is coming out of her mouth right now. Charlie has clearly pitted her against me.

"You, mister, are holding onto the past and you need to let it go! Have you ever stopped to think that maybe you misunderstood what happened last night or are you too stubborn to comprehend that you are the one who screwed up? Are you so quick to judge someone who may have also been through the same thing you have?" She exclaims loud enough I'm scared a nurse may come in here to check on us.

"What are you talking about?" I lower my voice so I don't draw attention to Hazel's room. "I already know Charlie has been cheated on in the past. All the more reason to be upset she was with Dane last night." I'm so confused. She's gone senile in this hospital.

"Maybe you're too absorbed in your own stuff you failed to see what was right in front of you. It's not Hazel's job to tell you what to do, but I will give you this bit of advice… You'll never have a good relationship with anyone until you let go of the last one."

"Hazel," I scoot closer to her in my seat. "He's taken a woman from me before and I'm not about to let that happen again. I wouldn't survive it."

"Then don't, my boy. Stop being so cold. That girl loves you. And you love her. Old Hazel knows and sees things that even you may not see." She smiles and pats my hand.

"Hazel, what do you know that I don't? I can't love someone I barely know." I beg her to answer me. I may be a fool, but I need to know what she's talking about.

"Oh, sweet boy, that's not for Hazel to tell. You can fix this. I know you can. Love doesn't work on your timeline. You need to stop standing in your own way." She continues to smile at me and squeezes my hand.

I suppose she's right. This is something I have to fix on my own.

"What are you waiting for? Go." she says, and with that, I kiss her on the cheek and leave. I need to find Charlie and I'm pretty sure I know where she is.

CHAPTER 31

Charlie

The bookstore is quiet today and I'm grateful. After last night and then talking with Hazel today, I'm not in the mood to make small talk with people.

"What do you want to do with this new shipment of books?" Nikki shouts from the front of the store.

"Just bring them back here." I can scan them in my office and avoid customers. Nikki walks in with the large box, barely seeing over the top of it.

"You can't just sulk back here in your office all day," she muses as she sets the box on my desk.

"And why the hell not?" I look up at her from resting my head on the desk.

"He will come around." She sets the boxes on the floor in the corner of my office and sits across from me.

"I don't know that I want him to. Honestly. It's getting too complicated at this point." I rub my eyes, trying to focus. "I should have told him sooner."

"Maybe so. But there's no point in playing the what if game now." She's not wrong, but all I want to do today is sulk. I need to figure out what the hell I'm doing here. I need to figure out what I'm doing with my life.

"Are you still going to go to the baseball thing with me this week?" she asks. "I know things are different now, but you don't have to talk to Dane. I would really appreciate you going with me. I hate all those corporate dickheads who only want to flaunt all the money they have."

"I promised you I would. I'll be there for you and only you." I can't break a promise to Nikki just because everything else in my life is a mess. That's not the kind of person I am.

"Thank you so much! We can get drunk by ourselves on Bradford and Swartz's dime. They can afford it." She claps her hands together happily.

Ding. The bell on the door rings. "I'll go." Nikki stands and exits my office to take care of the customer. Thank God I have her because I don't know what I'd do if I didn't.

"Charlie?" Nikki peeks her head around the corner of my office a few minutes later. "Um…Jude's here. He wants to talk to you."

Shit…I should have known better than to come in today. "Uh, okay…send him back." I can't avoid this forever. No better time than the present.

I stand, waiting for the inevitable confrontation that's about to happen. Nikki shows him into my office. He looks smaller than normal, more anxious.

"I'll just close this to give you two some privacy." Nikki says as she shuts the door behind Jude. He's definitely nervous.

"We should talk." He shoves his hands in his jeans pocket, and I can't help it when my breath catches in my throat at the sight of him. Ugh. The nerve of him to show up here looking so good after last night.

"It's fine, Jude. We barely know each other. You were right. Maybe this was a mistake." I sit, too shaky to continue standing.

"Oh…you think this was a mistake?" he asks, not moving from where he's standing by the door. God, he's gorgeous. Memories of our night together begin to cloud my judgment.

"You said it yourself last night." I point out.

"I know I said it…but…" He trails off.

"It's really fine, Jude. No worries, okay?" I can't keep torturing myself with this. He didn't want to take the time to hear me out last night and now I don't feel like explaining myself. I'm exhausted and just don't have the energy to do this today.

"Ok. I just…I'm sorry for how I reacted last night, I just wanted you to know that." He turns towards the door and pauses, looking back over his shoulder at me. "Call me when you're ready."

I slump my head back down on the desk after he leaves my office. I'm angry at myself for feeling sad that he's leaving.

Nikki knocks on the door frame. "Why didn't you just tell him?"

"Were you eavesdropping?" I raise my brow at her, scooting my chair away from the desk and leaning my head back.

"Of course I was, do you know me at all?" She smirks and sits across the desk from me.

"Honestly, Nikki, what's the point? I can't see this ending well at all. Why waste our time?"

"How do you know it's going to end badly? You're not a psychic. I see how he looks at you. Like he never wants to look at anyone else. Like no one else exists when you're in the room." She sighs and leans forward. "Listen, I know you've been through a lot in your past, and I know you're afraid. But, if anyone in this world deserves to be happy and have someone look at them the way Jude looks at you, *it is you.*"

CHAPTER 32

Jude

I'm picking up Hazel from the hospital today and she's been calling me non-stop since she got the all clear to come home. I had to make a quick stop at the jobsite before picking her up and I've got five missed calls from her just in that hour. I click the last missed call and Hazel answers on the first ring.

"It's about time. I've got things to do and I'm tired of being stuck in this place."

"I will be there in 10 minutes, Hazel." I shake my head. Such a stubborn old woman.

"I'm counting." She hangs up before I can respond. I just smile and shake my head again, placing my phone in the cup holder. I know she's going to ask me how things are between Charlie and I, and I'm not ready for that conversation. I told Charlie to call me when she was ready to talk and I'm sure she will, at least that's what I'm hoping for. I haven't laid eyes on her stunning face in over a week. It's been longer than I had hoped but if there's one thing I am, it's a patient man.

I pull into the hospital parking lot faster than I intended. I can see a nurse pushing Hazel out the front doors in a wheelchair.

"Finally," she chastises as I walk around the truck to open the passenger door for her. "Now dear, you can take this stupid wheelchair back inside." She motions to the nurse. I smile at her apologetically and mouth *I'm sorry* as I help Hazel into the truck.

"She's just doing her job, Hazel. Don't be so rough on her." I shut the door, not giving her time to argue with me.

The ride back to Hazel's is pretty quiet until we get closer to the farm.

"I've got a lot to catch up on being gone for so long. Winter is coming fast. I need to get stuff prepared for the goats and get their shed winterized. And I also need to visit the tax guys. I have to see if I can get an extension."

"You still need to take it easy," I say, glancing at her. "The doctor said your injury isn't completely healed just yet. So, if you need help doing something you need to call me."

The doctors said even though Hazel is up and moving, she needs to be careful. She has certain medications she has to take to prevent blood clots and they are afraid she could dislocate it again if she goes back to regular activity right away.

"And I want you to promise me you're going to take your medications," I add. "It's important to me."

"Yeah, yeah, dear. I know." She resumes looking out the window and I have a feeling she's not going to do what she's supposed to.

"About the tax payment, you don't need to worry about it anymore. Dane and I took care of it." I didn't want to tell her but she's going to find out eventually.

Tears well up in her eyes and she grabs my hand. "You boys didn't have to do that for me."

"Hazel, it's the least we can do for you." I squeeze her hand, knowing that every penny towards her farm is worth it.

After getting Hazel settled, I decided to run back into town and just grab dinner at O'Henry's. I don't feel like trying to find something at home and even though I usually prefer being alone, all this stuff with Charlie is starting to drive me crazy when I have time to just sit and think about it. I refuse to not give her the space she needs, but I can't deny how difficult it is. Luckily, the bar isn't too busy, but busy enough to distract me.

"What can I get you to drink?" the bartender asks as he wipes down the bar in front of me.

"Just a beer, and a burger and fries, thanks."

"Sure thing, I'll get that right in." He hands me my beer and I take a long sip. I check my phone again for any missed calls or texts from Charlie and come up empty handed. *Stop obsessing, Jude.* I could text her, just to let her know Hazel is home. That wouldn't seem weird, would it?

She cares for Hazel, after all, and has been visiting her frequently. I find her message thread and type out a message. I read over it a few times and hit send. Immediate regret washes over me. What if she doesn't respond? She would, wouldn't she? Especially if it concerns Hazel.

Ding. I jump, surprised by the quick response.

> Great news.

That was a short response. However, I'm not sure what I was expecting. Maybe I could respond with something about the motel to keep her talking. I think for a minute and decide to go for it. I don't have much to lose at this point.

> Do you have time tomorrow to talk about the motel?

My heart pounds in my chest waiting for her to respond. Of course I deserve the coldness, but part of me wishes I could just have a chance to explain to her why I reacted the way I did. Not that it excuses my behavior, but maybe just provide some understanding. I also want to give her the chance to explain. I should have given her the chance to explain what happened in the moment, and I regret not doing so with every fiber of my being. Maybe if I had, it would be she and I sitting here having dinner instead of me sitting by myself.

I turn my phone over, willing there to be a response but there's nothing. Instead, I jump when I feel a hand on my shoulder.

"Hey, Jude." Kelsey smiles and takes the barstool next to me. "I'm sorry I didn't reply to your text from a while back. It seemed like you were having an off day, so I didn't want to jump to any conclusions."

"I think I was pretty clear in my text, Kelsey. I'm not interested in being in a relationship." I tap my beer on the bar, signaling to the bartender to keep them coming. I don't want to be sober.

"You see, that's interesting…" She pauses and runs her finger down my neck and to my arm where she rests her hand on my elbow. "Because I heard you were here, not too long ago actually, with Charlotte Collins."

I tense up at her touch and the mention of Charlie, wanting to swat her hand away, and roll my eyes.

"Number one, that's none of your business. Number two, again, none of your business." I take a long swig of the new beer the bartender sat in front of me when the bell on the door rings behind me.

"Well, well, well, speak of the devil." Kelsey smiles, hand still on my arm, as I turn around to see Charlie and Nikki enter O'Henry's.

CHAPTER 33

Charlie

"You look awfully irritated for someone who doesn't care." Nikki teases as she drinks her beer seated across from me in our booth.

"I'm not irritated. I just find it funny that just moments ago he was texting me and all the while he was here at the bar with her." The nerve, I swear.

"You don't know that he's here *with* her. You were very upset that you didn't get the chance to explain yourself to him when you and Dane were in here talking and now, you're doing the same thing to him. How is that fair?" She raises an eyebrow at me, pointing out the obvious hypocrisy in my reasoning.

"And, also, I know Kelsey. She's like a fly on shit to any man that comes into this bar looking even a little bit lonely."

I guess she's probably right but there is so much going on in my life right now everything just seems to be getting too complicated, and I'm not sure how much more I can take.

"What do you suggest I do then? Reply back to the text he just sent me about the motel while I'm sitting in the same bar as him?"

"God, no, silly. Go over there and take your man away from her." She motions over her shoulder towards the bar where I can see Jude looking visibly ill over the fact that Kelsey is so close to him.

"What? He's not mine, first of all, and second, I don't even know how to do that." This is where I have no game. How am I supposed to stake claim over a man that isn't even technically mine?

"That man is yours, all you have to do is give in. Go over there and take him back." She stares at me waiting for me to make a move.

"And leave you here alone?" How rude would that be?

"I'm a big girl and I want to sit on your side of the booth so I can watch Kelsey shit her pants in public." She grins ear to ear, and it gives me confidence. I grab my beer bottle and get up.

"Fine." I smile and turn towards the bar to save Jude as Nikki moves to my side of the booth, taking her seat for the show.

It's not a long walk to the bar but feels like everything is moving in slow motion the closer I get to him. Kelsey is rubbing her hand up and down his arm, smiling and talking while he sits still as stone with his hands wrapped around his beer bottle. I would be lying to myself if I said that watching her touch him didn't infuriate me.

I make my way to the opposite side of him from where Kelsey is sitting and lightly touch the hair on the back of his head, twirling the little strands in my fingertips the way I know he likes. He turns his head towards me and smiles.

"Miss me?" I ask, leaning down and pressing my lips softly against his. *Oh, how I have definitely missed this*. I'm unsure if this man is mine, but anytime we touch I want him to be. I linger a little longer on his lips than I probably should, and in turn, he swivels on his stool towards me and places his hands on my hips, pulling me closer to him to stand between his legs, clearly not minding the attention.

"Very much so," he responds, running his hands up and down my torso.

"Can't you see we're in the middle of a conversation?" I hear Kelsey pouting from behind Jude. Neither of us break eye contact with each other.

"I think the conversation is over, Kelsey," Jude responds, grinning at me from ear to ear.

"You'll regret this, Jude." Kelsey turns on her heel and stomps towards the door, slamming it shut behind her.

"I'm so very sorry for the misunderstanding with Dane. I should have known better than to assume you were here with him." Jude runs his thumb over my cheek, grabbing the back of my neck with his hand and placing a small kiss on my lips.

Now is the time, Charlie. Tell him. "Dane is the person who cheated on me recently." I lean back against the barstool next to him but continue to stand between his knees. The look on his face could only be explained as confusion. "When I first moved to town, he and I dated for a few months. It wasn't serious, just casual. But, on his birthday, I went to surprise him at his office, and he was fucking his assistant on his desk."

Jude doesn't move. He just stares at me, searching my eyes and seeming like he's trying to find the right words to say. When he comes up empty, I decide to keep going.

"I didn't know you were his brother, well, at first I didn't. I found out from Hazel. I wanted to tell you the other night, but we were having such a good night I didn't want to ruin it."

He continues to sit silently for what seems like forever before taking both of my hands in his.

"Dane's assistant, Katie. She's my ex." He continues looking at me while I stay silent, processing the new information that is starting to make everything else make sense. It explains why Jude and Dane have such a large disconnect, why he reacted the way he did when he saw me with Dane and why he's so grumpy sometimes.

"I'm so sorry." It's all I can muster up at the moment and I don't think there really is anything else to say. How did I not put two and two together? We've both been through the same thing with the same two people. What are the odds?

"I'm becoming more grateful for it as time goes on. If that hadn't happened in the past, I wouldn't be here with you in the present." He runs his thumb across my cheek again and I can't help but melt into him when he kisses me. Damn I could get used to this feeling.

"There is one other thing though." I push away from him, hesitant to bring this up right now, but I need to be honest. "I promised Nikki I would go to the company baseball outing with her and Ben tomorrow.

I think Dane will be there. But I will be avoiding him like the plague. I'm only going to be there for Nikki. You know how those things go."

He shakes his head at me like I'm being ridiculous. "It's okay. I trust you. Clean slate from here. I was just being stupid. Sometimes I do that." He smiles at me again and I know exactly how he feels. Sometimes we all do stupid things.

"I see you two have made up." Nikki stands behind us, hands on her hips. "I'm going to head out and let you two have some time." She sets her empty beer on the bar top.

"Nonsense. You two came for dinner. We can catch up when we go over some things for the motel?" he asks again, reiterating his previous text message.

"Day after tomorrow work for you?"

"That works for me. I will see you then." He gives me a quick kiss on the lips, and I motion for the bartender to grab Nikki and I a couple more drinks as we head back to our booth.

CHAPTER 34

Alex

I've come up empty with all my research on this new number for Charlotte. I've come to the conclusion that it's not a wrong number. If it was a wrong number someone would have responded and questioned me. At least that's what I would have done. Which leaves me with two different options. It's either her number or it's not active. The messages say they're delivered, so, through process of elimination, the number has to be active, and I've found her. Even if it is just electronically.

Today we have our yearly outing for the company, so instead of spending my day locating Charlotte, I'm obligated to socialize and network with all these assholes who have so much money they don't even know what to do with it.

The conversations are boring and all they want to talk about is their next vacation or the yacht they are thinking about buying. Currently, I was stuck in a conversation with a guy who's buying his third house, in the Hamptons. Must be rough.

I've been stuck in an assistant position at Bradford and Swartz for the past year. I tried moving up at my last real estate firm, but I kept getting told I needed to work on my people skills. *Work on my people skills, my ass.* They were just threatened by my determination and drive to succeed.

I moved to Bradford and Swartz right after Charlotte ran out on me with the promise of opportunities for growth, and well, that's taking longer than I want.

"Can you take a group photo of us, Alex?" Gerard hands me his phone and gathers the group of rich pricks to stand with the baseball field in the background. Of course, they want me to take the photo and not be in it. I snap the photo and hand the phone back to him.

"I'll send it to you so you can post it on all our socials," he says. "Make sure you use our hashtag, so it shows up with all the other branch's photos as well."

"Got it." *Can't wait to sort through all of those later.* I turn around and head out of the suite. I've got more work to do.

After the outing, I start the same routine I do every night, with the exception of having to sort through all the photos from today and get them posted onto all of Bradford and Swartz's social media accounts.

Looking through the photos, I can't help but feel jealousy boiling inside me as I stare at the rich fuckers. That should be me. And, once I have Charlotte back, that will make it even more attainable. When she's back where she belongs, I will have everything I need to move up in the world.

I picture myself owning my very own yacht like half of the men in these photos do. Charlotte and I would have such a wonderful time sailing together. We would go port to port, living life to the fullest while visiting small coastal towns, as long as she does well with her re-training. She's going to have to learn some respect and obedience before I take her out in public again.

After sorting through the photos and getting everything tagged how it should be, I decide to peruse the photos from other branch's outings today. They are all reminiscent of the photos I took today. I wonder if those assistants had the same duties I did today. Get this, fetch that, take this photo, blah, blah.

New York branch, there's a bunch of rich fuckers there. They have the biggest market out of all of us. Portland, they are more medium sized but still look to have quite a bit of money tied up between all of them.

Houston, a fairly large branch. I used to want to work at that one until I met Charlotte. She refused to move to Texas, so we stayed in Nashville. It was the one time I let her decide anything and now I regret it. I should have known better. She said she'd never leave Nashville. Liar.

Cedar Valley, our smallest branch. I'm sure none of these assholes have third homes, probably not even second homes. They deal in smaller real estate than most of the branches, but I guess you need small business too.

"Wait a minute." I say aloud to myself. "You're fucking kidding."

I'd know that blonde bitch anywhere. Nikki. Of course, I should have known. *She's with Nikki.*

CHAPTER 35

Jude

The weather is changing quickly. I can feel winter approaching in my bones. We've got to get some final things taken care of for the motel and I'm anxious about picking up Charlie today. We dropped a lot of bombs on each other a couple nights ago but I'm feeling better after getting those out in the open, and I'm looking forward to moving on.

"Hey, Jude," Nikki greets as I enter the bookstore.

"Good morning, Nikki." I notice the table at the front that used to hold all of Hazel's soaps is completely bare. "What happened to all of Hazel's stuff?" I motion towards the empty table.

"We sold all of it again! That's the third time we've completely sold out!" she exclaims. "Hazel said she would call you to drop some more off. She must have not had time to do that."

"Wow. That's really awesome!" I mimic her excitement and my reaction is genuine. Hazel now has medical bills on top of her impending property tax payment, so every little bit helps right now. "How was the baseball outing yesterday?" I ask, trying to seem nonchalant.

She rolls her eyes as she places books on the shelf. "Oh, you know, a bunch of drunk, rich dickheads, like always. Nothing exciting though." She leans in and whispers in my direction. "Don't worry, I kept Dane away from her."

"Jude." Charlie walks out of her office and toward us at the front of the store. She's dressed in black leggings and an oversized sweater that hangs off one shoulder. If Nikki wasn't present, I would probably take her right here on the floor. It's been way too long since I've tasted her. *Snap out of it, Jude.*

"Charlie. Are you ready to go?"

"I am." She turns to Nikki. "I shouldn't be gone too long. Just call me if you need anything."

"I'll be fine. Don't do anything I wouldn't do!"

"It's getting cold." Charlie wraps her arms around herself in the passenger seat of my truck. "I really don't like winter."

"Well, that's how it is around here. Summers are super-hot, and winters are super cold." I smile and turn up the heat on the dash. "How did you end up in Cedar Valley if you aren't a fan of winter?"

She grows still and I can feel the tension change in the air just by asking the question, making me instantly regret it. "I'm sorry," I say. "You don't have to answer that."

"It's complicated but, essentially, because of Nikki. She's really the only person in my life who has constantly showed up for me." She pauses, twiddling her thumbs in her lap. "How's Hazel? I haven't gotten a chance to check in on her yet."

"I spoke with her on the phone this morning, she seems to be doing well. I just hope she's taking her meds like she's supposed to be. She's stubborn and that worries me." Hazel has been known to call doctors crooks and pill pushers, so I have no doubt she's going to be fighting taking those meds.

"Me too, I will try to get out there this afternoon when I'm done at the store and check."

"I'm sure she would love to see you." I agree with her, we need to be checking.

"Listen, about the other night." She starts, but I interrupt her.

"We're good. Don't worry about it."

"I know we are. I just feel like maybe we're rushing things a bit. We both are coming out of terrible relationships with trust issues. We hardly know each other. There are things, complicated things…" she trails off and doesn't finish her sentence.

"Oh..." I can't hide the disappointment in my voice. "I understand. I want us to get to know each other better. It's been so long…I mean…I care very deeply about you. I've never met anyone like you." I'm stumbling over my words like an idiot.

"I don't mean I don't want to keep doing what we've been doing," she says as she places her hand on my arm that rests on the console. "I just think maybe we should slow it down a bit. I feel the same way about you also, Jude. You're not like any man I've ever been with."

"I can be patient." While that may be true, I don't look over at her as we pull into the parking lot of the motel. Every time I look at her, that patience grows thin. I'm going to have to learn a little more self-control when I'm around her.

"What are we looking at today?" she asks as we walk into the lobby. "Wow, this looks great! The guys have been busy."

"Yeah, they have been. I think it's coming together nicely. The wood flooring was just finished yesterday but I wanted your thoughts on the decor in the lobby." I lead her over to the counter where I have some samples set out from the hardware store.

"What are these for?" She points at the different tiles laying on the counter.

"I was thinking of doing an accent wall behind the counter with one of these but wanted your insight. I want to have a sign with the motel name hanging there on top of whatever tile you think would be best." I point at the wall in front of us.

"I think since we have gone with so many neutrals you should go with this dark green stone. It will really bring out all the other textures and colors you have going on, and add a pop of interest for people when they check in. It looks natural but also high end." She taps her finger on the tile. I can't help it when the thought of grabbing her hand and sucking on her finger crosses my mind making my cock throb in my jeans.

"What's wrong?" she asks, bringing me back to reality and away from the thoughts going wild in my head.

"Oh…nothing." I rub my hand on the back of my neck trying to ease the tension growing within me.

"You seem tense." She lightly strokes my arm with the same finger I was imagining in my mouth just moments before. She gasps when I grab her hips and push her up against the counter.

"Listen Charlie. I told you I can be patient but if you keep touching me like that, I'm afraid I'm going to become very *impatient*." I push myself up against her and a small noise escapes her throat when she feels my erection pressing against her stomach.

"Oh…I see." She looks up at me through her lashes and runs her fingers up and down both of my arms. The little shit is taunting me on purpose.

"I'm warning you." I can't believe she just said she wanted to take things slow and here she is pushing all my buttons. Right now, her actions are saying completely different things than her words.

"Does this also make you impatient?" She moves her hands to my shirt and slips them underneath, running her fingertips along my back, sending shivers down my spine in the process. "Or this?" She moves up to her tip toes and brushes her lips across my jaw line. My patience is thinning, and she knows it.

A groan escapes my throat. "Not five minutes ago you said you wanted to slow things down." I brush my lips against her neck as she keeps torturing me. "I'm a pretty disciplined man, Charlie, but when you torture me on purpose, I find it very hard to remain that way."

"You're right. We should get going then." She pushes herself into me, her words not matching her actions once again. *Fuck this, we aren't leaving yet.* I spin her around so that she's facing the counter and push on the middle of her back so that she's bent over it.

"I warned you," I whisper, leaning down over her and kissing her shoulder exposed by the oversized sweater. "You wore this to torture me also, didn't you?" She nods her head. She knows exactly what she's doing. "And these leggings." I smack her ass. She jumps in surprise and whimpers below me.

I lean back down to kiss her neck when her phone dings on the counter beside her. I look over out of instinct and see the message on her screen, standing immediately when I see it's from an unknown number.

I found you...

"What the hell is that?" I ask, pointing at her phone. Who would be sending such ominous messages to her?

She jumps at my reaction and grabs her phone. The pink color on her face drains to a pale white. She stands motionless staring at the message and then up at me.

"Who is that?" I question her again.

"It's…no one…it's nothing."

"That doesn't look like nothing. Tell me what's going on." I demand. Why would someone be sending her messages like *that*?

"I've got it handled. I really don't want to involve you," she says, shaking her head and not meeting my eyes.

"Bullshit. Is it Kyle? I told him to leave you alone."

"No, it's not Kyle." She shakes her head again.

"Dane?" I'll kill him. Again, another head shake.

"Then who the hell is it, Charlie?" I'm becoming frustrated at this point.

"It's my ex, Alex. The reason I moved here. He was stalking me, and I reported it. The police said I didn't have enough proof. When I saw him lurking outside my apartment, I packed up all my shit and moved here." Her shoulders fall in defeat, and I feel a tinge of guilt for being so upset with her. But, dammit, how am I supposed to help her if she doesn't tell me what's going on in her life. "I got a new phone number but somehow, he tracked me down. Or at least it seems like he has."

"You need to go to the police with this." I point at her phone with the text message still unread on her screen.

"I've already got Detective Rhodes looking into it. He's got it under control." She shakes her head in defiance.

"Does he, though? Why are you still getting threatening messages if he's handling it?" Detective Rhodes needs to get his shit together. I don't see how having something *handled* results in messages like this.

"I don't know, but you're probably right," she says, giving in. "I should at least give him this message to trace."

"We're going to get this settled right now." I grab her hand and lead her out to the truck.

CHAPTER 36

Charlie - past

I got home from work late tonight, so I warmed up some leftover takeout and decided to veg out on the couch to catch up on some reality TV. It's a beautiful spring night so I open up the sliding door to allow the warm breeze to wash into the apartment.

I should be working on my bookstore proposal for the city, but I haven't had the energy with working double shifts lately. I spoke with Nikki on my drive home, and it seems like she's really enjoying her new life in Cedar Valley. The way she talks about the quaint little town makes me sometimes wish I had gone with her. But, I've got dreams of my own I'm chasing.

Luckily, over the past few weeks I have barely gotten any calls or texts from Alex. That means he's either given up or planning something terrible. I can't let my mind go there. I have to believe he's giving up. It's the only thing that keeps me sane. If I start thinking up all the crazy things he could be planning, I will lose my mind.

I'm taking a bite of my leftover takeout when I hear a noise come from outside. I pause with the fork still in my mouth and the nausea in my gut, that I haven't felt for months, returns. He's close. I can feel it.

I don't want to draw attention to the fact that I'm aware, so I get up casually and walk to my bedroom. There are no lights on in here so I can look outside without being detected.

I stand away from the window and scan the tree line behind my apartment for any sign of movement. My eyes finally adjust to the darkness and I see a figure standing amongst the trees. *Fuck. He found me.*

CHAPTER 37

Alex

It didn't take me long to figure out how far of a drive it is from Nashville to Cedar Valley. The bitch didn't go far, but it's far enough that I needed to leave immediately to get to her before she could run again. I've been in the car for four hours at this point and have a little over three left to go. I've only stopped for gas once and hope I can make it without having to stop again.

I know it was risky to send that text message, but I think I'm close enough now she isn't going to have time to go anywhere. If she's even getting the messages, that is. Thank God for Dane, whoever the hell he is, for posting that picture on the Bradford and Swartz hashtag or I might not have gotten this lucky break. Where there's Nikki, there's sure to be Charlotte.

I found a little cafe that is quiet and the perfect place to grab lunch undetected. If I know anything about Charlotte, it's that she doesn't trust the police anymore, so I wouldn't be surprised if she's trying to handle all these messages on her own. Good luck, my dear Charlotte. No one can save you now.

I did some research on Dane while I was waiting for my lunch. Luckily, for me, it wasn't hard to find information on him. I found tons of news articles about how he and his brother lost their father in a farming accident and then how their mother committed suicide in their barn not long after. He'll be my first point of contact when I get to Cedar Valley.

I've got three hours of driving to come up with a story to get him to help me. That's plenty of time.

CHAPTER 38

Charlie

I hate that Jude had to find out about Alex this way. It's just one more thing that makes my life so complicated and I hate dragging him into it. Inevitably, I know he will eventually get tired of all this and say to hell with me. I would if I were him.

He insisted on bringing me to see Detective Rhodes to show him the latest text I received. Alex has to be bluffing. There's no way for him to find out where I am. I made sure to cover all my tracks. *At least I thought I did*. Detective Rhodes stuck us in another sterile conference room while he took my phone to do a trace on it.

"How long has this been going on?" Jude asks, with more irritation in his voice than sympathy, and I can't help but feel a little disappointed by it.

"You mean this time or since it first started?"

"Both." He stares at me, emotion void on his face.

I lean forward and rest my forehead on my palms. Why does my life have to be so messed up?

"The first time, it started right after I ran out on him. This time, the night you kissed me at O'Henry's, the first time, in the hallway."

"And you didn't feel the need to tell me?" Now I can sense hurt in his voice.

"It's not that I didn't want to tell you."

"Oh, it's not? Because it sure seems like it. You've got someone stalking and harassing you, and you didn't feel the need to tell me you might be in danger?"

"I didn't want to drag you into this mess. It's complicated and potentially dangerous and you've got a lot going on in your life. I just didn't want to add any stress. You barely know me and I'm not your responsibility."

"Charlie." He turns to me and grabs both of my hands in his, finally showing emotion on his face. "You don't add stress to my life. I can protect you. I can help you. You just have to *let* me." He scoots his chair closer to mine. "You said earlier today that Nikki is the only person in your life that's ever been there for you. Let me be the second."

"I know." I smile at him, realizing that he's right. I need to let go and just let him. I feel so many mixed emotions with Jude. I feel guilty for dragging him into all of this but also grateful that he wants to help me. Our moment is stolen when Detective Rhodes walks back into the room.

"Well, good news is I was able to get one of my guys to trace the text." He rounds the table and sits across from us, sliding my phone back over to me.

"What's the bad news then?" Jude asks before I can.

"The bad news is the IP address I traced it to is from a diner in a town only three hours from here."

"Fuck!" Jude slams his hands down on the table and stands. "You can't go home. If the asshole is this close, he's not lying. He knows where you are and possibly where you live."

"That's ridiculous, Jude. I don't have anywhere else to go. Nikki will be there anyway, so I won't be alone."

"I agree with Jude, Charlotte," Detective Rhodes says. "It might be safer to stay somewhere else for now, until we can locate him. I've got a call out to a friend of mine up there who is going to work it from their end."

I can't believe these two ganging up on me. I do understand their concern but I'm so tired of uprooting my life because of this lunatic.

"You can stay with me on the farm. He won't know to look there. Let's go get the store closed up and get some stuff packed for you." He shakes Detective Rhodes' hand. "Thanks for everything. Please call us with any updates."

I realize it's pointless for me to argue, so I just stand and follow Jude's lead. Detective Rhodes follows us out of the conference room and down the hallway.

"Oh, and Jude...please don't try to take this into your own hands. Call us if anything goes awry at your place."

Jude doesn't answer the detective. He simply nods and walks out of the station with my hand in tow. I can't help but feel like if Alex showed up at Jude's house, the last thing Jude is going to do is call the police.

We stopped by the store and filled Nikki in on what was happening with Alex. She, of course, agreed with Jude that I should go stay with him on the farm.

"This is getting really old." I tell Jude as I throw clothes into a bag. "I've already had to uproot my life once because of Alex, I don't want to have to keep doing this."

Jude is seated on the edge of my bed and grabs my hand as I walk by to grab my stuff from the bathroom.

"Hey, it's okay. This is just for now. It's to keep you safe. I need you to do this for me. Let me keep you safe."

Let him. He keeps saying that and ugh if it doesn't drive me crazy knowing he's right, even if I don't like it.

"Fine." I begin grabbing all my stuff from the bathroom and throwing it haphazardly into the bag.

"I need you to tell me how dangerous he is. I know this isn't how you wanted to have this conversation, but I think it's important for me to know what we're up against." No, this isn't how I wanted to have this conversation at all but he's right. He should be informed.

I pause and stand in the doorway of the bathroom, fiddling with my hairbrush in my hands.

"He was very controlling. He told me how to act and dress, even how much makeup to wear. If I didn't do those things the way he thought they should be done, I would be punished. And, sometimes, even if I did exactly what he told me, I would get punished anyway."

"How?" he asks, concern lacing his expression.

"Hit, kicked, shoved, and sometimes he would force himself on me. The last time he did…" I trail off, unsure of how to tell Jude what happened, or if it's necessary. Maybe I should just keep my mouth shut. If anything is going to scare him off it's the fact that I stabbed another human being, even if it was just a tiny cocktail fork.

"The last time he did what?" He waits patiently for me to speak.

"The last time he forced himself on me…I…I stabbed him." I stand still waiting to see how Jude reacts to my revelation.

"Stabbed him where?" Oh geez, he wants details.

"I stabbed him in the leg with a cocktail fork I stole from a bar. Then I ran." My hands flop to my sides. He's going to think I'm crazy. This is where he's going to decide he doesn't want to help me anymore. "This is your out, Jude. I get how bad this is. If you want to run now, I don't blame you."

He stands from the bed and walks towards me, grabbing my face with his hands and staring me straight in the eyes with a fire I haven't seen before.

"I want you to listen to me. I'm not going anywhere. I will not let him, or anyone, do anything like that to you again. We're going to take care of this." His hands slide down my neck and to my arms. "Also, I will never inflict pain on you. Unless, of course, you ask for it. But, please, for the love of all things holy, don't stab me." He smirks when the words leave his mouth.

My lips part and a whimper escapes my lips. I can't help but feel guilty for how wet those words, and the thought of what Jude might do to me if I just ask him, make me.

What is wrong with me? Anytime pain has been inflicted on me I instantly have bile rising up my throat. When Jude says it, I can barely stand because of how weak my knees become.

He gives me a soft peck on the forehead before turning and grabbing my bag off the bed. "Finish up, we need to get going."

CHAPTER 39

Jude

Charlie is the last person I should have gotten involved with, at least that's what I thought at one time. I don't feel that way anymore. I'm all in at this point. I'm beginning to understand why she seems so anxious all the time, and why she's always fidgeting.

I'm fuming on my drive back to the farm and I'm glad Charlie isn't in the car with me. I need a bit to cool down after everything she just told me back at her place. If there is one thing I hate in this life, it's slimy men who prey on women.

I was young when we lost my father, but I still remember the values he instilled in me as a boy. You should always respect women and take care of them. And, under no circumstances, should you ever lay a hand on one. Unfortunately, for Dane, he was even younger and didn't get a chance to learn those values.

I can't believe she stabbed him with a cocktail fork. Note to self, never buy cocktail forks. I wish she would have stabbed him in the dick with it instead of the thigh. That would have satisfied me more.

I reach over and open the glove box, pulling out my handgun and checking how many rounds are in it. I haven't needed to use this thing in a while, but I will not be unprepared now, not when Charlie's life is seemingly at stake. I have no idea how dangerous this asshole actually is, but I refuse to take any chances. I tuck the gun in the back of my jeans. I don't want to scare Charlie by having it known, but I also need to be able to protect her if the time comes.

I can't help but smile at the way Charlie drives on gravel. You can definitely tell that it's not something she's used to. I fly down these roads at speeds that most would consider unsafe. I feel like Grandpa out for a Sunday drive following her.

When I see the farm in sight, I feel a tinge of relief wash over me. It's the one place I have always felt safe. I hope Charlie feels the same way.

CHAPTER 40

Charlie

It's been two hours since the text came through which means if Alex left the diner right after sending it, he could be in Cedar Valley within the hour.

Jude followed behind me in his truck back to his farm. He said we could park my car in the barn so that it wouldn't be seen from the road in case Alex did show up here. We pull into the drive, and I follow Jude down the pathway to the barn. He parks off to the side and opens the barn door for me. I roll my window down as he walks up to the car. "It might be a tight fit, but you should be able to squeeze in."

I look at him wearily and back to the very narrow barn door.

"Get out, I'll do it for you." he says, opening the car door.

The last thing I want to do is ruin his barn and my mind just feels like mush at this point. I grab all my stuff out of the back seat and stand to the side while he gets into the car and slowly pulls it into the barn.

Once my car is secured and hidden, we head inside to get settled. The house is just like I remember but there's a heaviness walking in this time.

"You can stay in the guest room if that makes you more comfortable." He points down the hallway.

"Okay." I'm not sure what would make me comfortable right now.

"Go get your stuff put away and I will figure out something to make us for dinner." He moves towards the kitchen as I head down the hallway to the guest room. It's smaller than his room. I sit down on the edge of the bed. What has my life come to? I keep running from everything, and every time I get comfortable somewhere, it all blows up.

"I know it's not much, but it's safe." I look up to see Jude standing in the doorway with a beer in each hand. "I thought you could use a drink." He walks towards me, hands me the beer and sits next to me on the bed.

"You thought right." I take a long swig of the beer and feel the coldness as it runs down my throat and into my stomach. "Thank you."

"I have some pasta I can make, if that sounds good to you."

"Honestly, I think I could just drink my dinner tonight." I smile at him, taking another long sip. "You're a great cook by the way." I waggle my beer bottle towards him.

He laughs at my comment and takes a drink of his own beer. "Well, then it's a good thing I have extras." We both finish off our beers pretty quickly in silence, just sitting next to each other. "Would you like another one?"

"I was thinking…" I grab his beer bottle from his hand, walk over to the dresser, and set them both down. I turn back to face him. "I would like to finish what we started at the motel when we were so rudely interrupted." I move toward him slowly, stopping only when my legs are on the outside of his while he remains seated on the bed.

"Oh, you would?" He looks up at me with his big green eyes and wraps his hands around my waist, moving them up the back of my shirt. I love the way his rough hands feel on my soft skin. He pulls me closer, and I sit on his lap, straddling him.

"I would." I smile, placing my hands on his chest.

He runs his fingers up the back of my neck and into my hair, clenching and pulling slightly as he presses his lips against mine. In one swift motion he flips us over and I'm lying on my back on the bed. It's hard to not want Jude especially after he finally knows my darkest secret and wasn't deterred in the slightest.

He pulls himself away from me and stands. "Then I guess you need to roll over." His eyes darken as he watches me. I keep eye contact with him as I do what I'm told and roll over to lay on my stomach on the bed. He grabs my hips and pulls me to the edge so that I'm bent over the bed.

"You want to finish *exactly* what we started?" He questions and I nod my head. "Use your words, baby."

"Yes." I struggle to speak.

"What do you want?"

I don't speak for a second. I'm a little out of my element. No one has ever asked me what I want before.

"Smack my ass." I mutter into the sheets.

He swiftly complies to my request, pulls my leggings down and removes them, tossing them to the floor. I feel his hand on my inner thigh moving up until his fingers find me.

"Mmmm, always so wet for me." He praises as he runs his finger up and down my slit, finding my clit and circling it. "If at any time you want to stop, just tell me."

I nod and turn my head to try and see what he's doing but am immediately scolded.

"No. Face down on the bed," he demands.

I do as I'm told, only able to hear what is happening behind me. I feel exposed and vulnerable in this position, but I don't hate it. I flinch when I feel the wetness of his tongue replace his fingers. He licks me up and down, continuing to circle my clit with his fingers. How does he make me want to come so quickly? Anytime I've been in this position before I hated it, but for some reason, with Jude, it's different.

Abruptly he stops and stands, and I can't help the whimper that escapes my lips in the absence of him. I hear him unzip his jeans and take them off. He grabs my hips and pulls me closer to the edge of the bed.

"All fours," he demands, and I do as he says. I feel the tip of his hard cock pressing against my entrance and instinctively press back into him. He stops me with his hands. "Nope. I'm in control. Make yourself come while I fuck you."

I move my hand between my legs and begin to circle my clit with my fingers as he pushes inside of me.

"Good girl," he praises my actions.

I feel every inch of him as he thrusts in and out of me. I position my hand between us and touch his cock that is now covered in my wetness, as he continues his rhythmic movements. I move back to my clit as I feel my orgasm building deep inside me.

"Jude." I moan.

"Keep going baby. Come with me." He continues to move in and out of me as I circle my clit with the same rhythm until we both give in to our orgasms. We fall onto the bed, both out of breath.

"Let me shower with you?" he asks, moving strands of hair out of my face.

I nod. I don't think there's anything I wouldn't let this man do.

CHAPTER 41

Alex

It was late when I arrived in Cedar Valley and the only motel in town is still under construction leaving me nowhere to stay. It's probably for the best, seeing as how I don't really need a paper trail connecting me to this shit hole town. I just want to get Charlotte and get the hell out.

I choose to park in an abandoned parking lot for the night and do a bit more research on my main contact in this town. Dane VanHoss. He's an agent with Bradford and Swartz. I plan to make a stop there first thing in the morning. Based on the picture he posted on social media from the company outing, I think he will have just the information I need.

While driving from the tiny ass diner to here, I was able to concoct a story that I'm certain will allow me to get information out of Dane. Seeing as how he lost his entire family to such a tragedy, he should have a soft spot for things related to family matters.

I close out of my internet browser and pull up the photos of Charlotte on my phone.

"My dear Charlotte, I told you if I couldn't have you no one else would. It's cute you think I was kidding."

Flipping through the photos, I can feel the anger growing inside me. I tried many times to get over Charlotte and find someone else. But there's something so addicting about the anger she fills me with. The anger that never ceases to make me hard as a rock.

CHAPTER 42

Jude

I've been lying here awake for hours, at least that's what it feels like. I roll over and check the clock on my phone. One in the morning. Ugh. I've got to get some sleep.

After Charlie and I showered, I ended up making us pasta. We were both starving at that point and needed something besides beer in our stomachs. After watching some TV, she insisted on sleeping in the guest room even though I asked her to stay with me. I understood, but now I'm lying here wondering if she's having trouble sleeping as well.

I've thought about checking on her more than once, but I also don't want to come off as clingy, so I have refrained from doing so. I know she's struggling right now, and I don't want to add to that. I roll back over and try to force myself to sleep. I finally feel like I'm drifting off but jump when I hear a scream. *I did hear that didn't I? Was I dreaming?* I sit in bed, trying to see through the darkness and hear muffled sounds coming from down the hall.

I swing my legs over the bed and rush to open the door, making the muffled sounds coming from Charlie's room louder. She must be having a nightmare. I quickly find my way through the darkness to her room where I can faintly see her writhing under the covers as the moonlight shines through the window. I rush to the side of the bed and sit next to her, touching her shoulders lightly so I don't startle her.

"Shhh, Charlie. It's a nightmare, wake up."

She jolts awake and sits straight up in bed, almost headbutting me in the process. Her breathing is heavy and erratic, and the sight of her chest heaving is not helping my mind stay focused. She places her face in her palms and starts sobbing.

"I'm sorry," she says, repeating herself over and over.

"Shhhh." I grab her and pull her onto my lap, tucking stray strands of sweaty hair behind her ears. "It's okay, I've got you." I don't ask for permission when I stand and carry her to my room, placing her under the covers and crawling in next to her.

Her heart is pounding out of her chest and her body continues to tremble. I cradle her into my arms and stroke her back slowly, attempting to calm her down. "It's okay. I'm here."

"Mmmm," she murmurs and snuggles in closer. I feel her heartbeat start to slow and her body relax after a few minutes. I close my eyes and keep her close to me. Maybe now we can both get some sleep.

◈

"How did you sleep?" She's snuggled up under the covers as I stand beside the bed with a hot cup of coffee. She rolls over and rubs her eyes looking confused.

"What time is it?" She sits up looking around the room. "Why am I in your bed?"

"You had a nightmare. I brought you in here. It was the only way either of us were going to get any sleep." I hand her the cup of coffee. "It's nine in the morning."

"I'm so sorry. I didn't mean to bother you." She takes a sip of the coffee and looks up at me through those lashes again, *dammit*.

"You didn't bother me at all." I pause and sip my coffee before continuing. "I need to run into town. Make yourself at home. Lock the door behind me when I leave. Don't let anyone in. Even if you know them." I grab my wallet and keys off the dresser and lean down to give her a kiss before I go.

"So, this is like a prison then?" she asks, turning her head before I can kiss her. "I'm not allowed to leave?"

"It's not a prison, Charlie. I'm trying to keep you safe here. Please let me do that."

"How is leaving me alone here going to keep me safe?" she questions me, clearly the caffeine is taking effect.

"He doesn't know me or where I live. Lock the door. Don't answer the door. I will be back in a couple hours."

"Jude..." she trails off, and now I feel bad for attempting to leave her here alone even though I'm just trying to do what's best for her.

"What, baby?" I sit down on the bed next to her.

"Please don't leave me here alone today. Maybe in a couple days, but not today. Give me five minutes. I can be ready quickly. I promise to stay out of your way," she says with a pouty face.

"What if he's in town and sees you out with me? I don't think it's safe to be traipsing around town right now." I argue.

"Can't we take back roads? I can wear a hoodie and hide my face," she mimics, pulling the strings of a hoodie. "You wanted me to let you keep me safe, this is me letting you."

"Fine." I give in. "Get dressed, we're leaving in five."

CHAPTER 43

Alex

I wasted no time arriving at Bradford and Swartz this morning. I have things to do and not a lot of time to do them. I was greeted by a pretty little assistant at the main desk who sent me right upstairs to Katie, his assistant, who informed me that Dane VanHoss was in a meeting at the moment. Of course he is…these fuckers are always in meetings.

I waited in the lobby for over an hour until the little dick head finally made an appearance. He's scrawny and the pompous vibe he's giving off makes me nauseous.

"Mr. Fortright, join me in my office." He greeted me with a handshake, and I followed him down the hall. These offices are definitely simpler than ours in Nashville.

He leads me into his office and points to the chair in front of his desk. "Have a seat." He rounds the desk and sits in his own chair. "What can I help you with today, Mr. Fortright? Are you looking to purchase property in Cedar Valley?"

"No, Mr. VanHoss. My business here today is a bit more personal." I sit up straighter in my chair to deliver my story with more finesse. "I'm looking for someone and it has come to my attention that you may be of assistance in that area. You see, I purchased an item from an estate sale not that long ago, and I believe the ancestor of the original owner has recently set up residence in your beautiful town. Seeing as how you probably know a lot of the residents here, I was hoping you could be of assistance in locating her."

"I see…" He sits up straighter in his chair, seemingly intrigued by my story. "And who might you be looking for exactly?"

"I'm looking for Nicole Wright."

After my very enlightening meeting with Mr. VanHoss, I decided to stop at the only place to eat in town. I haven't had anything to eat since yesterday at that shitty diner, and this shitty bar isn't much better. I don't know what I expected when traveling to the middle of nowhere, but it wasn't this.

I order food and sit at the end of the bar facing away from the door. I don't want to be caught by anyone that might recognize me, even if that would only be two people.

With the new information I received from Mr. VanHoss, it seems my dear Charlotte is behaving like a whore again and her friend Nikki is an accomplice in the whole matter. He informed me that Charlotte opened a bookstore and employs her nosy friend. *Of course she does.* I also learned that she was dating Mr. VanHoss when she showed up here and has since moved on to sleeping with his brother.

Charlotte and Nikki sorely underestimate the lengths I will go to, and now that I have a lot more information on the man Charlotte is fucking, plans have changed. They all need to be punished.

Screw the apartment back in Nashville, these lessons need to be taught here, in shit-hole-middle-of-nowhere, Cedar Valley.

CHAPTER 44

Charlie

The trip to the jobsite was quick, probably quicker than Jude intended, since I insisted he bring me along. The motel is coming along quickly, and it looks like Jude is going to be able to make his Grand Opening date that is approaching.

"I'm going to stop at the grocery store, but I want you to stay in the car and keep your head down. We don't need to risk you being seen out in public." Jude pulls into the parking lot of the grocery store and hands me the keys from the ignition. "Lock this when I get out and don't unlock it until I get back."

I take the keys from him and fumble them in my fingers. "Okay." I'm not even going to fight him over this. He's right, like always, and I need to just suck it up for a while until all of this blows over.

"I'll be right back." He leans over and gives me a peck on the cheek before exiting the truck. He stands outside of the door for a moment, ensuring I lock it behind him before he heads into the store.

I pull my phone out of my back pocket and dial Nikki, who answers on the first ring.

"Any news?" she asks, without even saying hello first.

"Nothing yet. I just wanted to check on you and the store." I continue fiddling with the keys in my hand.

"Don't worry about me or the store. I have everything under control. Ben is here with me today. He didn't feel comfortable leaving me alone either."

"That's good. I'm waiting for Jude to get done at the grocery store and then we're heading back out to the prison."

"It's a damn fine prison if you ask me," she teases, lightening the mood like always. I can't help but smile.

"Yeah, it's not so bad I guess." I see Jude walk out of the store with bags in tow. "Jude's back, I'll talk to you later. Thanks again for everything."

"No thanks needed. Stay safe and call me if you need anything." Nikki hangs up the phone and I unlock the truck for Jude.

"Everything okay? Who was on the phone?" He throws the bags from the store into the backseat and hops in the front next to me.

"Yeah, I was just checking in on Nikki and the store. She has Ben there with her, so that makes me feel a bit better." I hand him the keys and find a string on my sweatshirt to fiddle with instead.

"Maybe she should just close the store for a few days?" he suggests.

"I mentioned that yesterday, but she thought it was silly. It's hard to tell Nikki to do anything." I stare out the window as we head back to the farm. Nikki is right, if I have to be stuck anywhere, Jude's farm is the best place to be stuck.

"I got us stuff for tacos tonight. I hope that's okay. And…I replenished our beer supply." He reaches over and grabs my hands, forcing me to stop playing with the stupid string on my sweatshirt. "Everything is going to be okay. I promise."

"I know. I'm just ready for it to be over. I don't understand how they can't find him in such a small town. It's not like there are many places he wouldn't be seen."

"Don't worry. I plan on calling Detective Rhodes when we get back to the house and checking in on his progress." He squeezes my hand. It is comforting to know that he's on my side.

We drive past Hazel's and a tinge of guilt washes over me because I still haven't been able to visit her. "We should stop and see Hazel."

"I spoke to her today. She's good. I told her I would stop by in the next couple days." He pauses before continuing. "You need to stop worrying about everything and everyone else around you and focus on yourself. That's the most important thing right now."

I nod, knowing he's right, even though it feels foreign to me to just focus on myself and my needs.

CHAPTER 45

Jude

I made tacos for dinner, and we decided to have a makeshift picnic in the living room. As we sit on the floor across from each other at the coffee table, I can't help but ask a question that's been floating in my mind since she said something about it.

"Tell me why Nikki is the only person who's ever showed up for you."

She uncrosses her legs and pulls her knee up to her chest, grabbing her beer off the coffee table and taking a long sip. "That's a really convoluted story to be honest."

I wave my hands, pointing around the room. "Well, it appears I have some time to spare. Tell me."

She sighs, reluctant to speak. "Fine."

I continue eating my tacos, waiting patiently.

"I know what it's like to not have parents. I mean, not in the way you lost yours, but absent by choice. My mother got pregnant with me in high school. My father was never around, from what I have been told. One of my foster mother's said that he ran as soon as he found out my mom was pregnant." She runs her hand through her long dark hair and plays with the beer bottle in her hands.

"She was sixteen, unprepared, with no support at home, and no idea how to care for a child. She took me to parties, left me with strangers, and eventually got me taken away from her when she went to jail at 18 years old. I was two and was thrown into the foster care system. I bounced from house to house until I was old enough to be on my own. No one ever ended up adopting me. Nikki was my best friend all throughout high school. She had a good family and they treated me like their own. I spent a lot of time there and her parents helped me apply to colleges when it was time. I worked hard to get through college on my own, but it helped having Nikki there with me. I've never spoken to my mother, and I don't even know where she is. It's just not a relationship I care to have."

I ponder her words for a moment and understand now why she cares for other people so much more than she cares for herself. She never had anyone care for her, so in turn, she makes sure everyone else has someone that is looking out for them.

"That must have been rough, not having a stable home to feel safe and loved." I take a swig of my beer and finish the last bite of my taco.

"When I was really little, yes. When I got older and understood, I realized that wasn't who I wanted to be as a person, so it got easier. I never wanted people to feel sorry for me. I don't need pity from others."

She finishes the last of her beer and sets it on the coffee table. "Tell me more about you, Jude. I just gave you the cliff notes of my life story, it's your turn." She winks at me, and I smile at her even though my story is just as depressing.

"I had a really good childhood, even though I lost both of my parents. Dane and I were very lucky to have our grandmother and Hazel. When we lost my dad, my mother just shut down. I don't think she knew how to live without him. They were high school sweethearts and hadn't spent day apart since they got married. When she couldn't take it anymore, she decided to end it. I was angry at first, but as time went on, I grew to understand the love they had for each other was just too strong for her to move on. I think she knew we would be taken care of, and she was at peace with that."

"What about you and Dane? Besides the whole Katie thing, is there something else?"

I can tell she's worried about asking that question because she winces when the words come out of her mouth, but I feel a bit obligated to share with her after everything she's told me about herself already.

"Dane loved the farm when he was little, before everything happened. He was so young. I tried to protect him from it. I think he has resentment towards me for keeping things from him. I was just trying to do what was best for him. I was just a kid myself. I didn't know any better. As soon as he graduated, he left the farm and moved away. He went to college and then came back angrier than when he left.

I tried talking with him when he returned but he completely shut Hazel and me out. There wasn't much we could do after months of trying to reach out to him. So, we just let him be."

"Maybe someday you can reconnect? Maybe you can rebuild your relationship."

"I don't know. After all of that and then everything with Katie, I just don't know if it's possible." I worry that it won't ever happen. I have come to terms with that possibility and can accept it if that's the case.

She moves to her knees and crawls around the coffee table, sitting in front of me. "You're a kind man, Jude. You're loyal and deserving of all the good things in life. Look at everything you've overcome."

I look down at the floor feeling too vulnerable for this conversation. No one has ever said the things she says to me or looked at me how she does.

I grab her and pull her onto my lap, wrapping her legs around me. "I don't deserve *you*."

CHAPTER 46

Jude

After our conversation, tacos, and beer last night, we ended up in my bed again. I convinced her to sleep with me, pointing out she would most likely end up here anyway.

She looks so peaceful next to me, and I hate to wake her, but I don't want to wait until it's too late in the day to take care of this problem.

"Charlie, I need to run back into town today. We need to leave soon." I brush the hair off her face and tuck it behind her ear. I could get used to her in my bed every morning.

"You could go without me today. No one has even seen or heard from Alex, so maybe he's not even around here after all." She rubs her eyes and pulls the covers back up under her chin.

"Are you sure? Yesterday you insisted on coming with me." She reaches over and touches my face with her soft fingertips. It sends those same chills down my spine that I can't seem to get enough of.

"I'm sure. I will be fine. I will just make some coffee and read a bit while you take care of your stuff."

"Only if you're sure. I don't want you to do anything you aren't comfortable with."

"Really, it's okay. You won't be gone long anyway."

"I will lock the door when I leave. Do not open it for anyone. Do you understand?"

"Yes sir." She salutes me and giggles.

I kiss her on the forehead then grab my keys and wallet. I turn around when I reach the bedroom door.

"Maybe be naked when I get back."

Considering everything that has happened over the past couple days with Charlie, I haven't had a chance to check in on Hazel. I stop there on my way to town. I need to ask a favor.

I can see her sitting on the porch when I pull into the driveway. She waves at me as I park and get out of my truck.

"Morning, Hazel. How are you feeling?" I walk up the steps and sit in the rocking chair next to her.

"I'm feeling good, dear. And, before you ask, yes, I took my medicine." She rocks back and forth staring off over the horizon.

"Glad to hear it. Listen, I have a favor to ask of you."

"Anything, dear, what can I do for you?"

"Charlie is in a little bit of trouble. Her ex, the one she moved here to get away from, well, it was pretty bad, I guess. He's found her, at least we think he has, so she's staying at the farm with me until this all gets sorted out. If you see anyone drive past the house in a vehicle you don't know, can you call me?"

"You left her there alone?" She stops rocking and gives me an accusatory look.

"I'm not super worried about him coming out here. It's been a couple days now and we haven't had another threat. As far as I know, he has no clue who I am, but just in case, I would feel a lot better if you'd just call me. I should be back in a couple hours."

"Alright dear, I can do that. I will probably be sitting out here until then anyway." She smiles and sips her coffee.

"What, no *tea* this morning?" I tease, knowing she hardly ever drinks coffee.

"Doc said it wasn't a good idea with my new meds." She frowns but I smile, pleased she's following the doctor's orders.

"Good. I'm proud of you, Hazel." I stand and lean down to kiss her on the cheek. "I'll be back soon. Thanks for the favor."

CHAPTER 47

Charlie

After Jude left, I took a shower and threw on his robe I found hanging on the back of the bathroom door. He wants me to be naked when he gets back, so this makes for easy access. I made a cup of coffee and took it out to the back deck. I should be safe here at least. No one can see me from the road.

Nikki texted and said everything is going fine at the store and not to worry. I couldn't be more thankful. I don't like feeling like I'm in a prison here, but I also would be lying to myself if I said I wasn't a little bit scared.

I look out over the field behind Jude's house and see a couple of deer grazing in the morning sun. What simple lives they live, but how ironic they face the same problem I do right now.

They live in fear of stalkers each year during hunting season. They run, hide, and fight for their lives, just like I have been doing. The sound of my phone ringing makes me nearly jump out of my own skin. When I see who is calling, my stomach does a somersault.

"Detective Rhodes, do you have him?" I ask, hopeful for a release from this beautiful prison I've only had to endure for a few days. How ridiculous am I? I almost don't want it to end.

"Unfortunately, no. I received a call from my contact. They have reason to believe Alex is in Cedar Valley as we speak. They lost him when they were tailing him here."

"How is that possible? Why didn't they just pull him over and arrest him?" I stand, feeling panic rise in my chest.

"I'm working on getting the details on that, but my recommendation right now is to stay put where you are and don't go out and about."

"Have you called Jude?" I wonder if he's on his way home yet.

"I have not been able to get through to Jude, maybe you could try." Oh great, he has no idea. Shit.

"Okay. Please call me if you find anything else out." I hang up the phone, my heart racing and palms sweaty, knowing that Jude doesn't know this recent bit of information. The panic I felt rising just moments before is now a full-blown attack. I start taking deep breaths to calm myself.

I try to call Jude and it goes straight to voicemail. *Fuck.* Pacing the deck, I try to clear my head and think. Nikki. I'll call Nikki. She answers on the first ring.

"Are you okay?" She asks, frantically.

"Detective Rhodes called. He thinks Alex is in Cedar Valley."

"Fuck! At least you're safe with Jude."

"Jude's not here. He had to go to the jobsite."

"He left you alone?"

"It wasn't his idea. It's only for a couple of hours. But I can't get ahold of him. What should I do? Detective Rhodes told me to stay put but I've seen horror movies, and this feels wrong." I continue pacing the deck with Duke following on my heels. I guess it's true when they say dogs can sense things.

Nikki is silent for a minute. I can tell she's trying to come up with a plan. After a few seconds she finally has an idea.

"Go to Hazels. At least then you're not alone," she suggests.

"Okay, yeah, I could do that. I should walk through the back fields, so I don't get seen from the road."

"Yeah, good idea. I will send Ben to look for Jude. Is he at the motel?"

"He is. At least I think he should be."

"We will find him. Call me when you're safe at Hazels. Love you."

"Love you." I reply. The line goes dead, and I rush inside to change my clothes, Duke still on my heels. I don't feel the most comfortable putting Hazel in danger, Jude did ask me to stay put, but I have the worst feeling that I need to get out of here. If there is one thing I've learned over the last couple years, it's to trust my gut.

I quickly throw on a pair of leggings and realize I didn't pack any shirts when I was in a rush yesterday. I rummage through Jude's drawers, throwing stuff out like a burglar on a hit, and find an old band tee to throw on. I quickly put on my sneakers and try to call Jude one more time. Voicemail. I decide to leave one this time.

Jude. It's me. Nikki's sending Ben to find you. I'm going to Hazels. I know you said not to, but I can't stay here alone. Please call me. I...I love you.

With that I shove my phone in my back pocket and rush into the living room, checking the door, vaguely realizing I just told a man I barely know that I love him. Still locked.

I grab my wallet out of my bag on the entryway table and head toward the back door, running out as fast as I can and leaving Duke inside. I shut the door behind me, head down the stairs on the side of the house and into the back field.

CHAPTER 48

Jude

"Kyle, I already told you, you're not getting your job back." This is the last place I want to be right now, and this is the last thing I want to be doing, but the guys informed me that Kyle has been showing up to the jobsite almost every day looking for me wanting his job back.

"This is bullshit. I didn't know you had laid claim to Charlie when I was asking her to go out with me." He throws his hands up in the air and follows me out of the motel.

I turn quickly on my heels to look at him and point my finger in his face, almost touching his nose. "That has nothing to do with why you don't have a job anymore. You don't have a job because I don't employ assholes that rush women in the hallway of a bar. Don't step foot back on this property or next time I'll have you arrested."

I get in my truck and grab my phone out of the cup holder as Kyle speeds off in his car leaving a trail of dust behind him. Five missed calls, Nikki, Charlie, Detective Rhodes, *Fuck!* And a voicemail. I should have known better than to leave my phone in the fucking truck.

I immediately dial Charlie. No answer. I dial Nikki next. No answer. Detective Rhodes. No answer.

"Fuck! Fuck! Fuck!" I turn the ignition and throw the truck into drive, speeding out of the parking lot, much like Kyle did seconds before.

I cut the fifteen-minute trip back to the house in half. As I drive past Hazel's I glance over. She was supposed to call me if she saw anything suspicious, but she's not even out on the porch now like she said she would be.

I don't have time to stop and see what's happening, no one is answering their phones, and no one is calling me back, so I need to get home as quickly as possible. I speed into the driveway and up into the yard right in front of the house, throwing the truck in park and not bothering to turn it off.

"Charlie!" I call for her over and over as I run up the porch steps, turning the knob to go inside and quickly realizing the door is still locked. Shit. Instead of wasting time getting my keys out of the truck I rush around the back of the house to the deck and up the stairs. I notice a coffee cup sitting on the end table by the rocking chairs. What was she doing outside?

I swing open the back door, half pissed that it's unlocked, "Charlie!" No answer.

Duke comes running from the bedroom to greet me. I scratch him quickly. "Where's Charlie, buddy?"

I check every room of the house and notice that all the dresser drawers are pulled out and my clothes are all over the place.

"What the fuck happened in here?" I ask Duke.

I continue to call for her, finding her nowhere.

Fuck! He's taken her. Then, suddenly, an even more dreadful feeling washes over me when I remember I didn't see Hazel sitting on her porch when I drove by just a few minutes ago.

CHAPTER 49

Charlie

It didn't take me as long as I thought it would to run through the back fields to Hazel's house. I've never ran through fields before or jumped fences, but I guess a little adrenaline goes a long way sometimes. When I arrived at Hazel's, I found her on the front porch, and she quickly rushed me into the house.

"Jude said he told you to stay put, dear. I was keeping a lookout for him." She grabs me a drink out of the fridge and sits down with me at the dining room table, coffee cup in hand.

"No tea for you, Hazel? I ask, surprised.

"Doc says I can't." She shrugs and looks begrudgingly at the cup in her hand.

"Good for you, Hazel. I'm proud of you, and I know, I just panicked. I'm guessing Jude filled you in on the mess I'm in then?" I take a swig of my beer, trying to calm my pounding heart.

She nods. "Why did you panic, dear? Did something happen at the farm?"

"Detective Rhodes called. He thinks Alex is in Cedar Valley. I was afraid to be alone, and I'm sorry for bringing you into this. I just didn't know what to do. I tried calling Jude, but he didn't answer."

"Don't worry, dear. I don't think he would find you out here anyway. I'm sure Jude will call us back as soon as he can."

She reaches under the table and fiddles with the hem of her shirt, pulling out a handgun and laying it on the table. "Ol' Hazel also knows how to protect herself. Let's just sit here and try to take your mind off it for a bit." She never ceases to amaze me.

"I need to call Nikki and let her know I'm safe." I pull my phone out and dial Nikki's number. It goes straight to voicemail. She must be busy with a customer. I decide to just leave one letting her know I'm okay.

Hazel begins to tell me about how things are going since her stint in the hospital. She's telling me about how she's managing the farm while nursing her leg when I suddenly recall the voicemail I left Jude before coming to Hazel's.

"What's wrong, dear?" She places her hand on mine from across the table.

"Oh, it's nothing. I just remembered something I did when I was panicking and now, I'm feeling a bit embarrassed about it." I take another long swig of my beer but quickly jump to my feet when I hear the knob on the front door jiggle loudly.

In one swift motion, that I was unaware someone in Hazel's condition could accomplish, she stands and grabs her gun off the table, cocks it, and starts moving slowly towards the door, arms outstretched with weapon in hand.

"Hazel!" I whisper scream at her, knowing she shouldn't be trying to protect me. I'm a lot younger and nimbler than she is. "Let me do it."

She turns to look at me over her shoulder. "Have you ever handled a firearm, dear?"

I shake my head in response.

"Then I think it's best you let Hazel take care of this." She moves towards the door slowly. The only sounds are the creaking floorboards beneath her bare feet. The knob jiggles again and I freeze in place. Not wanting to move an inch and draw attention inside the house to whoever is on the other side of the door.

Hazel reaches the entryway, moving back the curtain with the barrel of her gun. She looks back at me and reaches down, turning the door knob to let Alex in the house. "Hazel, No!"

But it's too late, she turns the doorknob all the way and as the door opens, she turns to me and smiles.

CHAPTER 50

Alex

The Book Nook. I'm parked across the street of the bookstore that Charlotte owns. From here I can see inside perfectly, and I've been waiting forever for this idiot to leave the store. Nikki is standing in the back behind the counter, and this dumbass is just standing there talking to her. *Get your books and get out already. I've got shit to do.*

When I met with Dane VanHoss, he informed me that Nikki worked at the local bookstore just down the street from his office, which just happened to be owned by the one and only Charlotte Collins. How convenient for me. I figured I would have to do a lot more searching, but it worked out perfectly. Now I just need this customer to get out of my way.

Over the past half hour observing the two in the store, I would about bet that this person isn't a customer at all. Probably one of her many boy toys just hanging around and hoping for a piece of ass.

I pick up my phone and look through my pictures of Charlotte again. "Soon, my sweet Charlotte, we will be reunited."

I always get lost in the photos of her, thinking about all the things I want to do to punish her. I'm going to have to step up my game to really make her understand that she can't behave this way any longer.

I let my mind wander and almost miss the man leaving the bookstore. Interesting, he looks just like a guy in that photo that I found Nikki in. Now's my chance.

I wait and watch him walk around the corner of the block before pulling into the alleyway next to the bookstore. I exit the rental car, hiding my face with the ball cap I would never normally wear.

CHAPTER 51

Jude

I'm getting ready to knock on the door when it suddenly opens and Hazel is standing before me. "Charlie." I'm about out of breath but able to get her name out of my mouth.

Hazel opens the door wider. I see Charlie standing still as stone in front of me. Her shoulders visibly fall in relief, and I realize I've scared her.

"Charlie." That's all I can manage. She falls to the floor in a heap and begins sobbing.

"Oh, dear," Hazel says as she unloads the live round from the gun I didn't even notice she was holding.

I rush towards Charlie and pick her up into my arms while she continues to sob into my chest. "I'm so sorry, I didn't mean to frighten you."

"I thought you were him. And you didn't answer my calls." She speaks between sobs, and I feel like my heart is being ripped out of my chest. I've let her down and it's the worst feeling in the world. I should have made her go with me.

"I'm so sorry. I'll never leave you again." There's nothing more to say. I stroke her hair and try to calm her down. I can feel her relaxing in my grip eventually, and she feels more stable to stand on her own.

"Let's go home." I tell her before turning to Hazel, "Thank you for keeping an eye on her. Keep that gun close and lock the doors. Call me if you need anything."

Hazel nods and closes the door behind us as I get Charlie down the steps and into the truck. I'm never leaving her alone again. What a stupid mistake.

On the short drive back to the house, I can feel the energy in the truck change drastically. She's angry, and I don't blame her. We pull in and she's out of the truck before I even turn it off, slamming the door behind her.

"Charlie, wait." She doesn't, of course, and makes her way up the steps to the porch, becoming more frustrated when she realized the door is still locked.

"I have to unlock it." I fumble with the key in the lock. She doesn't respond to me, just continues to stand next to me with her arms crossed, not making eye contact. She's pissed. I can feel it.

I open the door for her. She tries to slam it in my face before I can enter. Instead, I catch it, grab her arm, and turn her around quickly.

"Look, I get you're mad, but taking it out on me isn't going to do either of us any good."

"You didn't answer your phone when I needed you. You told me to let you keep me safe and you didn't do that. You said you don't say anything you don't mean but I'm not sure if I believe that." She stomps towards the kitchen, opening the fridge door and then slamming it shut. I guess she just wants to slam things around now. *Thank God I don't own any cocktail forks.* I've had enough.

"Stop slamming shit. You're going to break something."

"Just leave me alone, Jude." She turns to walk away from me, but I move towards her quickly, grabbing her waist and turning her to face the wall next to the refrigerator. I press my body up against hers and lift her arms above her head, pinning them there with one hand. I brush her tangled dark hair off her neck, lean down and bite on the spot I know she likes.

"Need I remind you I asked you to go with me this morning and you insisted you would be fine and stay put?" I bite down harder, still speaking through clenched teeth on her flesh. "Imagine the horror that went through my mind when I got home, you were nowhere to be found and the bedroom had been ransacked like an intruder had been here."

She whimpers against the wall but has stopped fighting me. I can feel the anger subsiding the longer I press into her. "I told you I was sorry, and I meant it. I also meant it when I said I wouldn't leave you alone again. Now, do you believe me, or do I need to show you?"

Another small noise escapes her mouth.

"Use your words, baby." I press into her harder against the wall.

"Yes."

"Yes, what?"

"Show me."

CHAPTER 52

Charlie

In one swift motion Jude spins me around, lifts me off the ground, and lays me on the kitchen table. "Oh…" a small gasp is all that leaves my lips as I'm taken by surprise. I should not be this turned on by how aggressive he's being, but for some reason my body loves it.

"Why are you wearing my shirt?" he asks as he tugs it up and over my head.

"I didn't have any. I'm the reason the bedroom looks the way it does."

He stares down at me, making me feel more vulnerable than I would like. I was in such a rush earlier I didn't even have time to put on a bra. So, now I'm just lying here, sprawled out on his kitchen table completely exposed.

"Still stunning, even when you're a pissed off little thing." He traces a line down my collar bone and then squeezes my hard nipple between his fingers.

My mouth parts at his words and he quickly devours mine with his, searching for my tongue with his own. One of his hands is placed next to my head while the other begins lightly trailing down my side and finally ending up between my still clothed legs.

"Always so wet for me, even when you're mad."

Am I mad? Was I mad? I don't even know now. My heartbeat is pounding in my ears and all I can feel is the heat radiating off him like a blast furnace. It might be close to winter, but it feels like the damn Sahara Desert in this kitchen.

He stands above me again, this time exposing me more to the bright daylight by pulling my leggings off and tossing them on the floor. I reach for him out of instinct, but he pins my wrists to my sides on the table as he kneels between my legs. I whine when he won't let me touch him.

"Use your words, baby." Ugh, why do I have to speak when he knows exactly what I want?

"I want to touch you."

"Patience, baby. Patience." He's back between my legs, devouring me with his gorgeous mouth before I can say anything else. I have never had someone taste me so perfectly and with so much desire.

"I used my words, let me touch you." I try to free my hands from his grip but it's no use. He's so much stronger than I'm. I finally decide to give in and let him take me however he wants. He continues to lick and kiss me in all the right places, getting me so close to falling over the edge and then stopping right before I do. A moan escapes my throat and my body trembles on the cold, hard table.

He stands and lifts me off the table, throwing me over his shoulder and smacking my ass in the process. I moan in response, and he chuckles under his breath as he carries me down the hallway to his bedroom. I expect him to throw me onto the bed, but instead he carries me into the bathroom and sits me on the sink.

"What are you doing?" I ask, still sweating from the event that took place in the kitchen just moments before.

"I'm running you a bath."

"A bath?" I ask, confusion lacing my tone.

"Yes, a bath," he confirms.

"You can't just torture me like that and then expect me to relax in a bath."

"Don't worry, it's for me too." He smirks and begins running the bath water. Once he's satisfied with the temperature, he moves closer to me and stands between my legs as I sit on the edge of the sink. I run my hands under his shirt and up his back. His head falls on my shoulder and a relaxed groan escapes his throat. I pull his shirt up and over his head, tossing it to the side. Reaching down, I unbutton his jeans, hooking my fingers in the waistband and slipping them down his legs along with his boxers. His hard cock springs to life in front of me as it finally escapes.

I reach down and start stroking him slowly, rubbing his precum over the tip with each stroke. He keeps his head resting on my shoulder as he digs his fingers into my hips.

"Patience baby, I don't want to come yet." He moves away from me, grabbing my hips and standing me on the floor.

He turns off the water and gets into the tub, sitting on one side. I follow him and sit facing him, wrapping my legs around his waist, and pressing myself into his cock. I tease him by just slipping the tip inside and then pulling away a few times before he grabs my waist and slams into me as hard as he can.

My head falls back, and a moan escapes my lips as he begins to thrust in and out of me, water sloshing out over the edges of the tub. He holds onto my hip with one hand and moves the other to rub my clit with his thumb, circling fast and soft until I'm about ready to come.

"I told you I wouldn't leave you alone ever again and I meant it." He stares at me and his eyes darken. "Do you believe me now?" he asks as he continues to circle my clit and move in and out of me.

I nod my head in response. There are so many feelings my body is trying to process at this moment that I can't find words to speak. He shakes his head at me as if to tell me nodding my head isn't good enough.

"Use my words?" I manage to get out between thrusts. He nods in approval.

"I believe you." And with that, I fall completely over the edge at the same time he does. Sparks ignite the back of my eyelids as he thrusts into me a final time before his own release takes over.

As our breathing calms and our bodies relax, I lean forward and lay my head on his chest.

He strokes my hair and tucks it behind my ear. "Good girl."

CHAPTER 53

Alex

I need to make this quick since it is lunch time. I don't need more customer's showing up when I'm trying to get shit taken care of. I locked the door of the bookstore quietly behind me when I entered, but the stupid bell on the handle gave away the fact that I had.

I'm impressed with how this place looks for such a shit hole town. Charlotte has pretty good taste, though I hate to admit it.

I keep my head down as I make my way to the back of the store. I need to stay anonymous for as long as I possibly can. I notice a cell phone laying on the counter. At least it isn't within her reach right now. Stupid Girl. I snatch it up and shove it in my back pocket as she comes out of the back room.

Quickly, I turn and grab a book off the shelf, flipping through its pages as though I'm interested in it.

"Welcome to The Book Nook. Is there anything specific I can help you find?" Nikki greets me.

God, I forgot how annoying this bitch's voice is. I think quickly about how I'm going to play this and decide fast is best. I don't have time to fuck around. I close the book and place it back on the shelf.

Slowly I remove my baseball cap and turn to face her. "I think I just found it."

CHAPTER 54

Jude

After our bath, I convinced Charlie to take a nap while I cleaned up the mess she made when she was ransacking my drawers for a t-shirt earlier this morning. She's stubborn, but I finally got her into bed and tucked in. I think the adrenaline from the entire morning had worn off because she fell asleep as soon as her head hit the pillow.

While she was sleeping, I took Duke out to the backyard to play fetch. He's been kind of neglected lately with everything going on, so I thought he could use some attention.

I pull out my phone, tempted to call Detective Rhodes, however, I'm not super impressed with how he has been handling this situation, so I decide against it. Noticing the red dot on my phone app icon, I remember the voicemail from earlier that I neglected to listen to.

I click the icon on my phone and see it's from Charlie. Even though I know she's safe in my bed, the anxiety returns knowing that this was left when she was in full blown panic mode. I click on it and listen. Then I click on it and listen again. And again. Did I hear that right?

I jump, startled when the door to the back deck opens and Charlie emerges wrapped in a blanket. She sits in the rocking chair next to me. "Thank you for making me take a nap. I think I needed it."

"I told you so." I'm unsure if I should bring up the voicemail now or not. Should I wait for her to say something? Did she forget she even left it? I decide that right now isn't the time.

"How long was I asleep?" She wraps the blanket more snuggly around her shoulders and tucks her legs up underneath.

"Just a couple hours."

"Have you heard anything?" she asks, yawning.

"I haven't. It's kind of strange. I tried calling Nikki, Ben, and Detective Rhodes and no one has called me back.

"Now that you mention it, I tried to call Nikki from Hazel's and she didn't answer then either. I spoke to her when I was leaving here, and she said she was going to send Ben to find you since none of us could reach you."

I stop rocking in my chair as I start piecing everything together. "What if he didn't come here looking for just you?"

She stops rocking as well, a look of confusion on her face. "What do you mean?"

"I mean, what if he came for Nikki also?"

It all makes sense now. There's no way he could have located Charlie seeing as how she pretty much erased her entire life from the internet. Nikki, on the other hand, would have been a much easier find. And what better way to get to Charlie than to go through her best friend.

"We need to go to the store." I say as I grab my keys and wallet off the dresser while Charlie gets dressed. "That's where she was last, and I don't know where else to start since neither her nor Ben are answering their phones."

"What if we're too late?" she says as she hops around the bedroom trying to put on her leggings. "Think about all the time we wasted today!" She's shouting except this time it's not out of anger, it's panic in her voice.

"Everything will be fine. Don't panic. Deep breaths. We will find them." I move closer to her and grab her face in my hands. "I promise."

"I should have never taken that nap. I should have been more worried that I hadn't spoken to her earlier." She throws a hoodie over her head quickly.

"You can go on with the should haves all day but that's not going to do us any good right now. Let's go." We rush out of the house and into the truck. I throw it in reverse and at the same time reach over between her legs.

"What are you doing? We don't have time for that." She smacks at my hand while snapping her knees together and looks at me like I'm being ridiculous.

I move my hand to pop open the glovebox and grab my handgun out from underneath a bunch of papers.

"I wasn't trying to finger you baby, but if I wanted to, I could do it while driving."

Her lips part slightly at my words, and I can't help the shivers that shoot straight to my dick. I know the situation we're in isn't ideal, but her reaction makes me want to slide my fingers inside her anyway.

"Try calling Nikki again." It's probably pointless but it will keep her busy on the drive into town.

"She's not answering. I'll try Detective Rhodes." She dials his number and places the phone on speaker as I speed down the gravel road towards town.

He answers after one ring this time. "Rhodes."

"Detective Rhodes, it's Charlotte Collins. We can't get a hold of Nikki or Ben. We think Alex may have them. We're headed to my store right now to check."

"I'll meet you there." He hangs up without saying another word.

"I've tried calling him multiple times today, 'bout time he answered." What's that fucker been doing all day anyway. It seems he's been a step behind since this whole ordeal started. I don't know what he's been up to but I'm definitely not happy with the way he's been handling this. It might be time to just cut him out of this whole situation and take matters into our own hands.

"I just hope we aren't too late." She sits tensely next to me, fiddling her fingers in her lap like she does every time she's anxious and all I can think is, *same, baby, same.*

CHAPTER 55

Charlie

The number of times I have been in a vehicle flying down this gravel road with Jude driving is two too many. My anxiety is on full alert, and I feel like the shittiest friend in the world. I can't believe that I was lying on my back naked on a kitchen table while my best friend was potentially in danger. *You're a terrible friend, Charlotte.* Jude is clouding my judgment and I'm not sure how I feel about that.

I don't know if my heart can take much more today, it feels like it's going to explode out of my chest and into a million pieces. This is why I never focus on myself before others. If I had been focusing on Nikki and Ben instead of my own twisted desires, we may not even be in this mess. I endangered them and Hazel today, and if something happens to any of them, I don't think I will ever be able to forgive myself.

Jude reaches over and grabs my hands, willing me to stop fidgeting with them in my lap. I jerk my hands away quickly, not wanting his touch to cloud my judgment any more than it already has. He snaps his head quickly in my direction.

"Look, baby, if you want to blame me that's fine, but it's not going to stop me from taking care of you."

How does this man constantly know the right things to say? I don't speak for the rest of the drive. I stare out the window and silently hope for my best friend to be okay. She's strong. Stronger than I am. I feel like she could take Alex in a heartbeat. She's faced him before, just not physically.

As we get closer to town, I attempt to reach Ben again and the call gets forwarded to voicemail.

We pull up to the store in record time thanks to Jude's driving skills. He parks right out front and tucks his handgun in the back of his waistband as he exits the truck.

"Wait here," he orders.

"Not a fucking chance," I say, swinging open the door to the truck. I'm not waiting here while he goes inside.

"Get back in the truck." He points as if I'm going to listen. Not this time.

"Absolutely not." I don't move from where I stand on the sidewalk.

He shakes his head at me, giving in to my stubbornness, and moves to the door. He tries to turn the knob, but it's locked. I run back to the truck and grab my keys from my bag. Once inside, Jude canvases the store and finds it completely empty as Detective Rhodes finally shows up.

"You should have waited for me." Detective Rhodes states as he looks around the store as well. Pointless, Jude already did your job for you.

"No thanks. We don't need your help anymore." Jude motions for him to leave the store. "You've not been on top of this at all and now Nikki is missing. What have you been doing?"

"I'm doing the best I can with what little there is to go on, Jude, and I also warned you not to take this in your own hands." Detective Rhodes moves closer to Jude causing my pulse to quicken. What is it with these two?

I move towards the counter when I notice a small shiny object lying on top of it. *That's not...*

"Jude..." I manage, my voice shaking.

"What, baby?" He moves to me quickly as I point at the object I haven't seen in quite a long time.

We both stare at it, unmoving, as Detective Rhodes comes up behind us confused.

"A cocktail fork?" he questions.

CHAPTER 56

Alex

Nikki didn't put up as much of a fight as I expected, but a good tranquilizer helps. When I revealed to her who I was I quickly injected her, not giving her time to call for help. I was able to move her into the car parked in the alley quickly, just like I planned.

I couldn't be more pleased with how well things are going for me. Everything is lining up perfectly and things keep falling into my lap like they were meant to all along. It won't be long before Charlotte finds the little memento I left for her in her store. A little token of remembrance, if you will. I can't wait to see her face. Soon.

With the information I gleaned from Mr. VanHoss earlier this morning, I decided to completely change my plans. In order to get

Charlotte back, I need a bargaining chip for her and for the asshole she's shacking up with. Now, I have the perfect place to make that happen.

Just as I'm finishing hiding the car, the phone in my pocket rings an unfamiliar tone. I reach for it and realize it's the phone I stole off the counter at the bookstore. When I turn the phone over to see who is calling, my smile widens at the sight of the name "Charlie" on the screen.

CHAPTER 57

Jude

What kind of sick fuck keeps the item their ex stabbed them with as a damn trophy? I'm not sure Charlie realizes how dangerous this guy is. It takes someone with a really fucked up mind to think that way.

I allow Detective Rhodes to bag up the cocktail fork for fingerprinting even though I'm still not happy with how the situation has been handled. I might be able to shoot people, but I don't have any way to run a fingerprint. Plus, it gets him out of our hair for a while.

Charlie is visibly shaken by the presence of the cocktail fork, and I can't blame her. I can't imagine the amount of trauma it brings back to the surface, especially seeing it on the counter of her store. I sit next to her on the plush couch to try and calm her down when my phone rings.

Quickly, I reach into my pocket and pull it out, only to see it's Dane calling me. I don't have time for his stupid shit right now, so I send it to voicemail and turn back to her.

"Why is Dane calling you?" she asks, still fiddling with her fingers in her lap.

"I don't know, but I'm not worried about it right now." I tuck her hair behind her ears and run my thumb along her jaw. "It's okay, we're going to find her. I promise."

"You can't promise that, Jude." She's doubtful of me and I completely understand. I have let her down way too many times recently for her to trust my promises. I only hope, once this is all over, I can prove to her I'm worthy of her. However, I wouldn't blame her if she decides I'm not. My phone rings again on the coffee table.

"Just answer it," she says with a sigh, and I hesitantly pick up the phone.

"It's not a good time, Dane." He begins talking quickly before I can hang up. I try to take in everything he's saying without missing anything, but at the pace he's speaking, it reminds me of when he was little and in trouble.

"You did what?" I shout louder than I intended, but I can barely believe what I'm hearing. He continues to explain himself and I cut him off. "Come to Charlie's store. You are going to tell her in person."

I hang up the phone and look over at Charlie. She looks so innocent, and her big blue eyes are welling up with tears again.

"Don't cry, baby."

"What was that about?" she asks, trying not to let the tears fall.

"You'll find out soon enough. Let's take some deep breaths." I breathe with her while we wait for Dane to arrive. He's got some explaining to do and she deserves to hear it straight from his mouth.

We don't have to wait long for Dane to come walking through the door of the bookstore. I smile at the relief on her face when she notices Ben walking in behind him.

"Ben!" She squeals and runs to him, hugging him tightly. "Wait, where's Nikki?" Her excitement is soon gone, and concern laces her features again, pinging me right in the chest.

"She sent me to look for Jude but when I got back, she was gone and so was my phone that I left on the counter. I ran down to Dane's office because I figured he had Jude's phone number."

Dane runs a hand through his dark hair knowing he has got more explaining to do than Ben. I still can't help but see that little boy when he does that.

"I think Dane has a few things to add?" I nod my head towards him while Charlie looks at me in confusion.

"I…um…well, I may have given Alex some information today about you and Nikki." He shuffles back and forth on his feet, visibly shaking.

"You what?!" She screams at him and lunges forward, hands outstretched. Before she can get to him, I wrap an arm around her waist and stop her.

"Let me go!" She struggles in my grasp, but I don't let loose.

"Listen to what he has to say." I tell her as calmly as possible. Looking back at Dane, I warn him, "I'll let her go if you don't get to it."

He throws his hands up in submission and begins speaking.

"This morning I had a guy come into the office. He said that he had recently purchased an item from an estate sale that he believed to be a family heirloom of Nikki's. He seemed believable so I just told him that she worked at your bookstore."

"Are you fucking insane!?" She screeches and tries to remove herself from my grasp again. I hold on tighter, letting him continue.

"How was I supposed to know you had a stalker? You never mentioned that to me before!" He gets defensive and takes a step back, clearly afraid of what Charlie might do to him if I let her go.

"Having a stalker isn't something you just go around telling people! You should have never given out information about either of us! Now she's missing and in danger, all because of you!" She's fuming and I can't help but be a little turned on by it.

"I think I might know where he took her though." Dane tries to relax but doesn't break his eye contact with Charlie.

"How would you know that? He couldn't have been stupid enough to tell you," she snaps.

"He didn't tell me exactly, but I just spoke to the receptionist in the main part of our building. She said she overheard a man walking out earlier talking to himself mumbling something about Jude and a barn."

My eyes darken at the thought of my barn and what it means. Charlie relaxes in my grip. I feel comfortable enough to loosen my hold on her.

"How would he know the significance of the barn?" she asks. "That makes no sense."

"If you google our names, stories from then come up from old newspaper articles. He could have gotten it from there. And, if he knows you and I are together, he could be trying to get revenge on us both." I offer her an answer to allow Dane to relax. I'm proud of him for coming and admitting what he did to her in person. Maybe there is hope for him and me yet.

"Okay, then why the fuck are we all standing around here. Let's go!" She moves out of my hold quickly and gets in the truck before we can even get out of the bookstore.

This woman is determined, and damn, if I don't admire that.

CHAPTER 58

Alex

After hiding the car and getting Nikki's deadweight body into the barn, I was able to get her up into the hayloft, just like the newspaper articles I found described. I'm lucky I had a rope with me just in case or this plan wouldn't have come together so perfectly. It's not hard to find videos on the internet teaching you how to tie a noose.

I've been waiting for a few minutes, hoping Nikki wakes up in time to not miss out on all the action. I'm sure someone will be arriving soon, and I want her awake for the show. I walk over to where she's propped up against the beam in the loft and kick her thigh.

"Wake up," I demand.

She stirs and mumbles something intelligible through her duct taped mouth. I kick her again, this time harder.

"Wake up, Bitch. The show is going to start soon."

She opens one eye, then the other, looking around the barn quickly trying to figure out what's happening. I laugh and walk to stand behind her.

"You're the reason this all had to happen, Nikki." I lean down and get close to her ear. "If you would have just stayed the fuck out of my business, we wouldn't be in this situation."

I move to stand in front of her. She looks at me with tears welling up in the back of her eyes, unable to wipe them off with her hands tied behind her to the beam. She looks down, noticing the rope hanging around her neck. She starts to writhe and move around, trying to free herself. Her muffled screams make me smile.

"No one's going to hear you, Nikki." She jerks her body again, this time with more force. "Be careful, Nikki. If you move too much you might fall over the edge, and I'll have to just cut the ropes holding you up here. We don't want to start the show before everyone arrives."

She looks at me in horror. The difference between her and Charlotte is when Charlotte looked at me like that, it made me hard. Nikki doesn't make me hard at all. I can't stand this bitch and I can't wait to watch her eyes bug out of her head when I finally push her over the edge.

"You're the reason Charlotte wouldn't obey me. You're the reason Charlotte stabbed me, and you're the reason my dear Charlotte ran away from me. Well guess what, Nikki? I came to take back what is mine and get rid of you once and for all. You're not good for Charlotte. You only poison her mind with lies and deceit."

I begin to walk behind Nikki again, nudging her back to scare her a bit thinking I'm going to push her over. Right before I nudge her again, I hear a car door from outside the barn. I turn to Nikki and smile.

"Showtime."

CHAPTER 59

Charlie

"He's not answering!" I've been trying to call Ben's phone for the past five minutes we've been driving, hoping to get ahold of Alex and talk some sense into him before he hurts Nikki.

"I don't think he's going to. We just have to hope we aren't too late." Jude tries to calm me with his words, but it is no use. I won't be calm until I see Nikki and know she's okay.

Ben and Dane are in the truck behind us, and for two guys who don't drive on gravel much, I'm happy they're able to keep up. I'm still fuming at the fact Dane gave out so much information about Nikki and me to a complete stranger, but it's hard to place all the blame on him since I never mentioned Alex to him. He had no idea he was leading a stalker and potential killer to us.

"Listen, I don't think he's going to hurt her yet. What leverage would he have if he hurts her before we even get to him." Jude makes a good point I didn't think about amid all this anxiety.

"Right. Yeah, you're probably right. He's trying to teach you and I a lesson, he needs her to do that." I try to reason this has to be the case. If he's hurt one hair on her head, I will kill him myself. I've stabbed him before. It wouldn't be hard to do it again.

When Detective Rhodes left the bookstore with the cocktail fork to do the fingerprint analysis, I told him I didn't need it. I knew exactly who that fork belonged to. He insisted he take it to the station and Jude didn't argue. I just think Jude wanted to get him out of the way. And now, we're headed back out to Jude's farm with no backup from the police, prepared to handle this all on our own. I don't doubt that if Jude gets the chance, he will kill Alex.

"You're going to kill him, aren't you?" I ask him for confirmation, I need to hear him say it.

"I will if I have to, and I won't think twice about it." He continues to look forward and drive, not flinching at the thought of murdering another human being. I feel like I should be afraid of that, but I'm not. It's actually comforting to me, but I decide I will process that later.

"What if you go to jail?" I know I have been angry with him multiple times over the past few weeks, but I don't want him taken away from me. He might piss me off, but I don't want to be anywhere but where he is.

"Don't worry, baby. Let's just get this over with." He reaches over and squeezes my fidgety hands, and I sit up straighter in my seat as we get closer to the farm.

We fly past Hazel's house and I only hope she isn't sitting on her porch watching all of this take place. I could see her trying to come down here to see what's going on and that's the last thing we need her to do in her condition. She might think she's feeling better, but her hip is still in recovery, and we don't need any setbacks in that department.

The bile begins to rise in my throat the closer we get to Jude's farm. It's the tell-tale sign that I'm getting closer to Alex. It always happens when I'm near him. I wish I would have kept that fucking cocktail fork. At least I could have had some sort of protection if I needed it. Jude has a gun, and I just have to depend on him to protect me. I remember the pepper spray in my bag and reach down, fumbling for it.

"What are you doing?" Jude asks, glancing at me as he begins to slow the truck down and pull into the driveway.

"Getting this." I pull out my pepper spray and show it to him proudly. He just shakes his head at me as he turns into the driveway.

"Fuck!" he shouts, loud enough to make me jump and look forward at what has his beautiful eyes as big as saucers. Ahead of us, parked in front of the barn, is Hazel's old truck.

CHAPTER 60

Alex

I can barely contain the excitement that boils inside me when I hear the car door shut outside letting me know my dear Charlotte has finally come back to me. I take my hand gun and shove it in the back of my pants to climb down the ladder that leads up to the loft.

"I'll be back, Nikki." I warn her as I start to climb down, her eyes still full of tears, filling me with joy.

As I reach the bottom of the ladder, the barn door slowly creaks open. I can't wait to see Charlotte's beautiful face. It's been so long. As the figure silhouetted by the light outside the barns comes into focus, I realize it's not Charlotte at all.

I reach back to grab my gun when the voice of an old lady shouts at me.

"Don't move, sonny, or I put a bullet right between your eyes." I stop immediately and keep my hands at my side. She moves closer to me. I realize she also has a gun, and it's pointed straight at my face.

"Who the fuck are you, old lady, and where the hell did you come from?"

"Ol' Hazel doesn't like little boys who treat women poorly." She slowly moves towards me with the agility I wouldn't expect from someone of her age.

"Listen, lady. This doesn't concern you. Put the gun down. I don't want to have to hurt you." I put my hands up in front of me. I can take an old lady. I don't know what she thinks she's doing putting herself in this situation. She must be senile.

"I warned you. Don't move." She repeats herself like she thinks it's going to stop me. "Now drop your gun on the floor. I'm sure you have one. And don't try any funny business or Hazel will shoot." Why the hell does this lady keep talking in the third person? She's fucking crazy.

I reach behind my back slowly, just in case this psycho decides to fire, and grab the gun out of my waistband. I decide now is my moment. There's no way she'll actually hit me. I whip the gun out of my waist band and turn it towards her to shoot. The gunshot rings in my ears and I realize, the sound didn't come from my gun. I fall backward, and as I hit the ground, my vision goes black.

CHAPTER 61

Jude

What the fuck is Hazel doing here? I throw the truck into park and don't bother turning off the ignition. Charlie and I hop out at the same time as Dane and Ben pull in behind us.

"Why the fuck is Hazel's truck here?" Dane shouts from behind me as he jumps out of the vehicle.

"I don't know." I yell at him over my shoulder as we all rush toward the barn. We're almost to the door when a gunshot rings out from inside the barn.

"Hazel!" I hear Charlie scream from behind me. No. No. No. Please don't let Hazel be dead. I repeat over and over to myself as we reach the barn door. Everything has turned to slow motion. I can only hear muffled screams and words around me as the blood pools in my ears. If she's dead, I'll never forgive myself.

I reach the door just ahead of everyone else, opening it farther than it already is. When I do, the inside of the barn becomes soaked in sunlight, and it takes me a minute to process what I'm seeing.

Hazel is standing in the middle of the barn over a man's body, pointing her gun straight at his head. I can't tell if he's dead or alive. I hear muffled cries coming from above and look up to see Nikki tied to the beam in the loft, a noose around her neck and duct tape on her mouth.

"Nikki!" I hear Ben shout from behind me as he rushes towards the ladder to the loft, climbing it faster than I ever have. I look behind me and Charlie is walking slowly towards Hazel and the man lying on the ground. Dane walks up to stand beside me. He looks as dumbfounded as I feel.

"Hazel, did you kill him?" Charlie asks quietly as she kicks him in the side, seemingly trying to see for herself if he's actually dead.

"Oh, no dear. Hazel warned him though. I just shot him in the gut, shouldn't have hit any vital organs. And, if I did, well then, whoops." She lowers her gun finally and turns to face Dane and I. "Hello boys, it's about time you showed up."

"Jesus, Hazel, you could have been killed." Dane speaks up before I can, but he took the words right out of my mouth.

"You boys act like I can't take care of myself, and I'm starting to get offended." She smirks at us, and I can't stop the laugh that escapes me. Hazel never ceases to surprise me. That's for sure.

Ben unties Nikki and removes the tape from her mouth. Once she's down the ladder Charlie runs to hug her.

"I'm so sorry. This is all my fault." Charlie sobs into her best friend's shoulder.

"I'm fine thanks to Hazel. She's amazing with that gun. I definitely wouldn't want to run into you in a dark alley, Hazel." She laughs as we all stand around still trying to process the events of the day.

"Someone should probably call an ambulance." Hazel pipes up. "You know, they take a while to get out here."

"Yeah," I agree. "We probably should."

"Do we have to?" Nikki asks.

"Yeah, are you sure?" Charlie asks in agreeance.

"Unfortunately, we do." I would prefer to let this asshole lie here and bleed out but, we have to make some attempt to get him medical attention. Once that is done, we will seek the justice Charlie and Nikki both deserve.

"Why are you even here, Hazel?" Dane asks and now that he says it, I'm wondering the same thing again.

"I saw a suspicious car drive by. I knew something was up. So, I came down here," she says, shrugging like it's no big deal when, in fact, it's a huge deal.

"Hazel, I asked you to call me if you saw something suspicious, not take matters into your own hands." I shake my head at her knowing full well I shouldn't be surprised. Hazel never listens.

"Potato, Pa-tah-to, my dear." She smirks back at me.

I turn to Charlie and grab her wrist, spinning her towards me.

"Hey, I forgot to tell you something."

She looks up at me through those lashes again, "Hmm?" "I love you, too." She blushes as the words come out of my mouth. I lean down and kiss her softly, hoping she can feel that I mean it.

CHAPTER 62

Charlie

The paramedics arrived to take Alex to the hospital about a half hour after the incident occurred. Hazel was right, she didn't hit any vital organs, so Alex should be healthy enough to face trial for the slew of charges that are now pending against him.

Once Hazel was settled back at home, and Nikki was checked out in the emergency room, Dane asked if we would all be up for having dinner together at O'Henry's tonight. It was hard to say no when I saw Jude's eyes light up with hope at his brother's request. As much as I resent a lot of the things Dane has done in the past to both Jude and I, I want nothing more than to be supportive of their future relationship, if it's something Jude wants.

O'Henry's is buzzing tonight with talk of everything that happened earlier in the day. We can barely have a conversation because of the amount of people coming up and asking for details on what happened.

Dane, Katie, and Ben are seated on one side of the table while Nikki, Jude and I are on the other. Our waitress takes our menus from us as Dane pipes up from the end of the table.

"Can you just keep the beers coming for us, it's been a long day."

We all laugh, as does the waitress. "Absolutely."

"So, this is kind of awkward." I acknowledge as everyone sits in silence. Jude places his hand on my thigh under the table.

"To get it out of the way," Katie says, speaking up finally after being the most silent at the table. "I just want to say again that I'm very sorry to both of you for the things that have happened in the past. But, I'm grateful for the chance to do this with all of you."

Jude waves his hand, "It's okay." He looks over at me and smiles. "If all that shit hadn't happened, we wouldn't be here today." He raises his beer, and we all follow his lead.

"To the future," he toasts.

"To the future," we all repeat, raising our glasses in unison.

"So, what's next for the VanHoss brothers?" Ben asks as he takes a long pull from his beer. Jude and Dane look at each other for a brief moment when Dane finally speaks up.

"I was thinking I might like to invest in the motel project, that is, if you'll have me?" He looks to Jude for approval, and I squeeze Jude's hand under the table, giving him mine.

"I think that's a great idea." Jude smiles and looks down the table at Ben. "What's next for you, Ben?"

Ben fidgets in his seat for a moment before scooting his chair back and getting down on one knee in front of Nikki at the end of the table. Her mouth drops open and her hand flies up to cover it. I slap her leg and squeeze.

"Oh my god." I can't help it when the words come out of my mouth. Everyone at the table, and the entire bar, falls silent as Ben begins to speak.

"Nicole Ann Wright, from the moment I laid eyes on you I knew that you were the one for me. Your kindness and compassion towards others, and your not-give-a-shit attitude, are some of the things I love most about you. Every adventure we've shared and every challenge we have faced have proven to me that I do not want to do this life without you. I have never been more certain, and especially after today's event's, that you are my person. When I thought I would never see you again, I thought my life was over." He reaches into his pocket and pulls out the most gorgeous ring I have ever seen and holds it in front of her. "Will you do me the incredible honor of becoming my wife?"

Nikki is visibly shaking as tears stream down her face. Hand still covering her mouth she begins to nod quickly, answering him with a silent yes. He slides the ring on her finger and pulls her up to kiss him. The bar erupts into cheers.

"A round for the house!" Ben shouts.

I stand and wrap Nikki in my arms. "I'm so happy for you!" I squeal as I hold her tight. She deserves the world and I'm so happy she has found Ben to share that with. "Let's celebrate!" Everyone stands and congratulates Ben and Nikki as the music on the jukebox plays a familiar tune.

Jude turns to me, "It's the first song we danced to."

"It's the only song we've danced to." I lean into him as he takes my face in his hands and kisses me deeply.

"Well, do you want it to be the second song we dance to?" he asks with his lips still pressed against mine.

"I do." I smile up at him and he gives me a look that says he understands my choice of words. As he leads me out to the middle of the floor, I look around as my heart swells with joy. I never wanted to come here. I felt like I was running away from everything my entire life. Trying to find something else, something better, something stable and something safe.

Now I realize that all along, I was trying to find a place to call home.

As I watch the people most important to me dancing alongside us, I can't imagine home being anywhere other than here, in Cedar Valley, in the middle of nowhere.

EPILOGUE

1 year later

"I can't believe you are married!" I'm helping Nikki change into her dress for the wedding reception as her sister, Emily, is pouring us another round of champagne.

"I can't either!" Emily says, as she hands us each our glasses. "A toast. To the best sister and friend a girl could have." We raise our glasses and clink them together in unison, giggling as we sip.

The wedding was beautiful, even for a winter wedding. I hate the cold and told Nikki she was crazy for wanting to get married in the middle of snow but, when she wants something she goes for it. I can't help but admire that about her.

Jude and I were part of the wedding party and man does he look delicious in his tux. A far cry from the jeans and t-shirts he normally wears. Dane and Emily were the Best Man and Maid of Honor, both of them looking stunning as well.

Nikki chose an ivory-colored, floor length satin gown with a low back and crystals that adored the bottom which sparkled like the snow around her. She looked like a snow princess.

"Are you ready to go back to the party?" We finish off our glasses of champagne in the room at the motel we used to get ready. Jude was kind enough to let Ben and Nikki get married at the motel, which he coined *Margaret Manor*, after his mother.

"Emily, fill us up and we will head out there." Nikki laughs, handing her glass back to Emily for her to top it off. With full glasses in hand, we make our way back out to the small ballroom of the motel.

I search around the room, looking for my handsome date, and find him in the corner talking with Mr. Wright, Nikki's father. He catches sight of me from across the room, causing Mr. Wright to look my way, as well. As I make my way toward them, I see him say something to Jude but am unable to hear him over the music coming from the DJ booth.

"There she is," Mr. Wright says as he pulls me into a hug. "We've missed you so much, Charlie."

"I've missed you too, Mr. Wright." He kisses me on the forehead before letting me go. "I hope you're not scaring him off." I nod towards Jude.

"Not at all, my dear. Just making sure he's taking care of my girl." I'm so thankful to have Nikki's parents in my life. They are pretty much my parents as well, and it feels good to have them in the same place I call home now.

Soon after Ben's proposal, he moved in with Nikki. I wanted to give them their space and Jude offered for me to move in with him. We both agreed it was soon but at the same time there was nothing else we wanted more. This was it for us and we both knew it.

Alex was found guilty on all counts against him and is to be sentenced later this month. There's so much hope in feeling vindicated for something you knew to be true even when no one else believed you. I look up at Jude, so thankful for the life we have been creating here together.

"Dance with me?" I ask him.

"I'll always dance with you." He smiles and leads me out to the dance floor.

"Are you happy?" he asks as we sway in time with the music.

"Mmmm…very." I snuggle in close to him and we almost make it to the end of the song before he leans down and his hot breath dances across my ear.

"Wanna find somewhere quieter?" He kisses right below my earlobe, knowing it sends a shock wave straight to my clit.

"Right now?" I tease. He knows I'll go anywhere with him.

"I've been waiting all night to get under that dress." He leads me off the dance floor and down the hall to the room we booked for ourselves for the evening.

We don't even make it to the room before he slams me against the wall and devours my mouth like his life depends on it. I used to worry about people witnessing our little shenanigans, but I have come to not care. He lifts one of my legs up around his hip and presses his growing erection against me. He slides his hand under my dress and up my thigh finding how wet I'm for him. It always makes him groan, although, I don't know why he seems so shocked, he knows that I'm constantly ready for him at all hours of the day.

"Give me all of you, Jude." I breathe out as best I can.

"Right here? In the hallway?" he questions me but I know it excites him just as much as it excites me.

"Yes, please." I can't wait any longer. If he wants to take it slow, we can accomplish that later.

"Yes, ma'am," he responds, wasting no time unbuttoning his slacks and pulling out his hard cock. I pull up the hem of my dress to give him better access and, seeing as how I opted for no panties, he should have no issue finding me.

He pins me up against the wall harder and thrusts into me in one quick movement, making my breath catch in my throat. He circles my clit with his thumb like only he knows how to do while he pumps in and out of me. We continue matching each other's thrusts until I'm on the verge of coming undone all over him.

"That's it baby, give it to me." He continues circling my clit and presses harder as I finally unravel all over his cock. Sparks ignite in my vision as I feel him pulsing inside of me. We both take a minute to catch our breaths and come down off our highs. He kisses me softly before setting me down on my feet. As I pull my dress back down, I can feel his release running down my inner thigh and can't help but smile knowing it's all mine.

He's finishing getting himself back together when we hear footsteps racing down the dim hallway towards us.

"Charlie, I've been looking for you." Emily is out of breath once she reaches us and takes a minute to gather herself.

"What's wrong? Is Nikki okay?" I ask, placing a hand on her shoulder.

Through panting breaths, she manages to get out, "There's a woman at the coat check. She says she's your mother."

ACKNOWLEDGEMENTS

First and foremost, I need to thank my husband, who probably against his better judgement, encourages me to follow all of my wild and crazy dreams. THANK YOU, Trav, for allowing me the safe place to be me.

Secondly, I want to thank my kids for cheering me on even though they aren't allowed to read what mom writes.

To my Beta readers: Maria, Jess, Shawna, Britney and Taletha. Your encouragement and constructive criticism made this book what it is today.

To my badass line editor and sister, Shawna. Thanks for showing me that I have no clue how or when to use commas. It's a good thing I have you to double check my work and I am so grateful for the time and effort you put into this novel.

To all my new readers, thank you and welcome! I hope to continue to bring you stories that make you feel all the things.